WOODMILL HIGH SCHOOL

BIRTHDAY

BLUES

Anne Cassidy

■SCHOLASTIC

Scholastic Children's Books,
Commonwealth House, 1-19 New Oxford Street,
London, WC1A 1NU, UK
a division of Scholastic Ltd
London ~ New York ~ Toronto ~ Sydney ~ Auckland
Mexico City ~ New Delhi ~ Hong Kong

First published in the UK by Scholastic Ltd, 2005

ISBN 0 439 96325 7

Typeset by M Rules
Printed and bound by Nørhaven Paperback A/S, Denmark

10 9 8 7 6 5 4 3 2 1

AUGUST 20th

The baby was found outside a doctor's surgery. A little boy, only a day or so old. He was fast asleep in a cardboard box. It wasn't a chilly morning but he was well wrapped up anyway: a babygro and fleecy top; a stretch cap and mittens and soft woolly socks. It was all in different shades of blue. All brand new, just like the baby.

A policeman noticed the box by the garden wall. It was sitting on the pavement, in full view. He'd been driving past at just after six on his way back to the station. It was a gloomy day, with rain specks in the air, the clouds fat and heavy. He'd glanced at it, slowed down and then reversed back. It had taken a moment to register what he'd seen.

"I thought it was a pet," he explained to the duty sergeant. "That's why I went over. I thought it was a puppy or a kitten, something nobody wanted. I never dreamed. . ."

The baby was in a pet carrier. Plain brown cardboard with handles. The policeman, Robert Mathews, picked the box up with great care. He held it underneath, afraid that it might tear or give way. He needn't have worried. The baby was newborn; only six pounds two ounces in weight.

1

"The funny thing was," he said to the nurse at the hospital, "when I was bending over, looking at the little thing, I had this feeling that someone was *watching* me. Then when I straightened up and looked around there was nobody there."

The nurses named the baby. They called him *Bobby* after the policeman.

CHAPTER ONE

This story starts just as another one ends. My seventeenth birthday. The afternoon of the twenty-fourth of February. I was standing on the footbridge over the motorway waiting for Ben. It was our usual after-school meeting place, away from the school gates and prying eyes. Underneath me were six lanes of speeding cars and I bent forward to feel the air rushing past. A few moments later Ben came along and finished with me. There was no little speech, no sad face, no *Let's stay friends*. Just a few curt words, while he picked at the zip on his jacket and looked uncomfortable. Then he turned and walked back along the footbridge, speeding up as he got to the end where his mates were standing waiting.

I stood absolutely still, my hands in the pockets of my jacket. I'd been expecting a present and a card. A birthday kiss. Not to be casually dumped. It couldn't have taken more than twenty seconds for him to

3

deliver his words and then walk off. I was stunned. I turned my face to the road and watched the never-ending stream of traffic flash past. It seemed to blur, one car morphing into the next. I looked back along the footbridge, up to the road that led to the school. There were kids in uniform milling round. I thought they were looking at me but most of them were youngsters playing around with each other. That's when Tina Hicks saw me. She hesitated for a second and then came over, her enormous rucksack making one of her shoulders slope down. I edged away. It wasn't as if she was a friend or anything.

"Are you all right, Julia?" she said, raising her voice above the noise of a stream of lorries.

I nodded and walked off, leaning forward so that my hair covered my face. The last thing I needed was a nice, dull, *fat* girl feeling sorry for me.

Ben Holland had been my first real boyfriend.

We'd been a couple for ten weeks. We got together at the Christmas party. Ben came straight over when he saw me and asked me how I liked my work. I thought he meant my A levels.

"No, in the Willow Tree?" he said.

Most weekends, I worked with my mum as a waitress in a restaurant attached to a pub. I had to wear a daft uniform but the basic pay was good and the tips were brilliant. I earned much more than my best friend, Sara.

"How did you know I worked there?" I'd said, surprised.

"I have my ways, Miss Diamond," he'd said laughing, his hand slipping round my waist.

After that it had been easy. A few drinks, a couple of dances, a walk outside, a pause to kiss up against the brick wall of the senior common room. Over his shoulder I could see into the darkness, the pinpricks of lit cigarettes held by the other kids dotted around. He was a serious kisser, his lips and teeth pushing against me, his hands rubbing across my chest and neck, his leg edging between mine. Afterwards, I'd walked home with Sara, hugging myself with pleasure, still feeling my skin tingling from his touch. For ten weeks I was his girlfriend. The best time of my life.

I walked off the footbridge and went along the road that led home. When I got to the corner of my street I felt suddenly lightheaded and had to lean against a garden hedge.

"Are you all right?"

I could hear Tina Hicks behind me and felt her hand lightly on my shoulder. Where was Sara when I needed her?

"I'm fine," I said, shaking her off. "There's no need to follow me!"

Tina Hicks wasn't following me, I knew that. She lived across the street from my house, had done for months. She was a *friendly* sort of girl and sometimes, when Sara wasn't around, we walked to school together.

"Have you fallen out with Ben?" she said.

I nodded.

"Where's Sara?" she said, frowning.

I shrugged my shoulders. That was it. I needed to speak to Sara. She would know what to say, how to handle the whole situation. I pulled my mobile out of my pocket and jabbed at the buttons. The ring tone sounded, but then the voicemail clicked in.

Hi. It's Sara. Leave a message.

"Her mobile's switched off!" I said, through my teeth.

"Shall I go and find her?" Tina said.

I nodded, gratefully, and she turned and walked back towards the footbridge and school. Like I said, Tina Hicks was *nice*. Just not my sort of friend. I watched her go and then sat down on my front garden wall.

"It's getting too serious," Ben had said. "I can't see you any more."

How could he have said such a thing? My throat felt tight and I tried to swallow back a few times. I got my house keys out and used them to jab at the bricks beneath me.

A door opened at a house across the road and Tina's mum, Marilyn Hicks, came out. She walked to her gate and looked up and down the street. She was waiting for Tina, I knew. Her long hair was loose and she was wearing a brightly coloured blouse that looked silky and cold and a short skirt and boots. Even from that distance I could see her make up: red lipstick and thick tan-coloured foundation. She looked edgy, her lips moving as though she was talking to herself. She glanced in my direction and I gave a little wave. I felt a moment's sympathy for Tina. It was bad luck to have a mother who tried to dress like someone half her age. It was embarrassing.

Just then Tina appeared, on her own, at the corner of the street. My chest tightened up. How could I have expected her to find Sara? She didn't hang around with any of the kids I knew! Why should she know the places where we sat, the shops where we lingered, the bus stops where we chatted? I sighed, wishing more than anything that Sara hadn't had to rush off at the end of class to see a teacher about her coursework.

Marilyn Hicks looked visibly agitated and raised her hand in a jerky wave. Tina called something to her and headed across the road towards me. She was puffing, her face red from rushing. I should have felt grateful, instead it irritated me. Why didn't she just lose a bit of weight? I stood up, letting my bag drop on to the ground. I clutched my keys tightly in my fist, feeling the serrations digging into my skin.

"Couldn't you find her?" I said.

"I did find her," she said, glancing back to where her mum was.

"Couldn't she come?"

"I didn't speak to her," Tina said, pursing her lips.

"Why not?"

I raised my voice. I couldn't help it. At that moment it seemed as though it was all Tina Hicks's fault. As if my woes and troubles were her doing.

"She was busy. She was with Ben Holland."

I smiled. It was going to be all right. Sara would talk to him, make him see that he'd done the wrong thing.

"That's good," I said.

"Thing is," Tina went on, "she was *with* Ben Holland. She was kissing him."

Kissing him. Sara and Ben Holland. My mouth went dry and I bit hard into my lip. Tina went to say something but I shook my head. She hesitated for a moment and then turned away, back towards her mum.

Sara and Ben. The strength left me and I sat back on the wall. It was my birthday, and my boyfriend and my best friend had got together. At that moment I thought that nothing so bad could ever happen to me again.

But I was wrong. There was worse to come.

CHAPTER TWO

I rushed into my house and slammed the front door as hard as I could. The floorboards vibrated beneath my feet. I knew there was no one in so I slung my bag on the stairs and sat down and cried. On the hall table I could see a number of white envelopes, the kind that usually held birthday cards. I ignored them and went up to my room. When my mum finally came home she brought with her the smell of fish and chips. It drew me downstairs, and I told her everything in a few garbled sentences.

"But I don't want to talk about it and I don't want a thing to eat," I added.

"Right," she said.

"Because it's too upsetting to discuss," I said.

She put some chips on a plate and pushed it in front of me.

"It's too painful," I said, clearing my throat.

Then she put a piece of fish and the rest of the chips on her plate and started to eat it. I watched her taking mouthful after mouthful. Then I picked up a chip and fed it into my mouth in an absent-minded way. Her knife and fork was scraping at the plate.

"You're hungry," I said. It sounded like an accusation.

She stopped and looked up at me.

"I'm sorry you've broken up with Ben. He was a nice lad. But don't pick a fight with me. Especially on your birthday. It's a kind of special day for me as well."

"It's a birthday I won't forget in a hurry."

I stood up leaving most of my chips uneaten, and went out, grabbing the edge of the door as though I was going to slam it. But it was only half-hearted and it just clicked shut behind me.

In my room I sat with my mobile on my lap half watching TV. For hours I waited for the ring tone or the beep that told me I had a call or a text. About ten I heard my mum coming up the stairs.

"I'm having an early night," she shouted.

I heard her moving about in the bathroom and then in her room. I went along the hallway and knocked on the door.

"I'm sorry, Mum," I said, sitting on the edge of her bed.

"Never mind. It'll be bad for a while but you'll get over it. It's all part of—"

"The rich tapestry of life blah blah. . ." I finished her sentence for her.

She gave me a kiss and I went to bed.

I stayed off school the next day. When I finally got out of bed I found a Post-it stuck to the hall mirror.

Kath's coming for tea tonight. She's got a prezzie for you. Be nice to her. Luv Mum X

I groaned. The marvellous Kath. My nineteen-year-old cousin who was just finishing her first year as a nurse. What an absolute saint! It was all I needed. I went back to bed, burrowed down under the duvet and closed my eyes tightly. It wasn't long before I started thinking about Ben Holland.

The night of the party had been a real surprise, like an early Christmas present. We'd stood outside the common room and in between kisses we'd talked. Just remembering it made my throat feel sore. We'd swapped family history. I'd told him about my mum's job as a manager at the Willow Tree and the fact that my dad had left when I was still a baby.

"My dad's a teacher," Ben had said, breathlessly.

Everybody liked him. Loads of girls wanted to go out with him. He had chosen me, though, and I felt privileged. When his hand slipped under my jumper and rested on top of my bra I swallowed a couple of times with nervousness. He kissed me then, his mouth barely touching mine, his hand like a feather across the lace of my underwear.

Why would I say no? I wanted him.

I got up, pulled my jeans on and found a T-shirt

11

and jumper. It was only ten o'clock and I had a desire to be in school, sitting next to Sara, making notes from the white board and whispering gossip about the other kids. Sara, my *best friend*.

I made my bed, shaking the duvet with some force. I used my fists to pump up my pillows and then kicked some scattered shoes underneath. Sara and me had been best friends for over a year. Ever since she'd changed forms and ended up sitting next to me. We hit it off immediately. We both liked the same clothes and music and television programmes. We looked similar as well. Both of us were small with fair hair. Hers was long, though, and she was always doing things with it, plaiting it or curling it. Mine was jaw-length and hung with a slight curl which my mum said she liked. Some people said we were like sisters.

I sat down on my carefully made bed and felt this heaviness inside my chest. I tried to think hard about her hair. How had she had it the previous day? It had been loose, hanging around her face, glossy and thick. She'd been wearing mascara as well, I remembered noticing it; the contrast between her thick black eyelashes and her honey-coloured hair. How could anyone mistake us for sisters? She was nicer-looking than me, clear skin, straight shoulders, bigger breasts. Those things shouldn't matter, but they did.

And now she had Ben Holland.

About twelve, when I knew the bell for the end of morning classes had just rung, I got a phone call. I let the answering machine take it and as soon as the message light started flashing I pressed the button. *Let it be Sara*, I said to myself. The voice, when it came, was croaky and hesitant.

Hi Julia. I mean, this is a message for Julia. It's me, Tina. I was ringing to see . . . I was just phoning to make sure you were all right. . ."

I pressed the *delete* button. Not Sara. Or Ben for that matter. Neither of them were sitting holding their mobiles regretfully, trying to get back in touch with me. Just Tina Hicks.

I ate a sandwich and watched daytime TV. At just after four the doorbell sounded. I turned my head towards the front window, a feeling of gloom in my stomach. I didn't expect it to be Ben or Sara. The whole day of silence might as well have been a whole year. It was over. It was gone. As I got up and walked towards the door I knew who I'd see there. Standing awkwardly, her giant rucksack pulling her shoulder down. Tina.

"Are you all right?" she said, her face crumpled up with worry.

"I'm fine," I said, holding the front door half shut.

"Sara gave me this."

Tina was holding out an envelope. The sight of it made me feel nauseous. I could see Sara's handwriting.

Julia Diamond. Formal, as if it was an invitation. It was underlined, making it look as though she was determined that I would receive it. I held my hand out weakly and took it.

"See you then. . ."

I closed the door and with clumsy fingers I opened the envelope and pulled a sheet of paper out.

Dear Julia, it said, *I'm really sorry that things didn't work out between you and Ben. I don't want you to think that him and me were together for ages. It wasn't like that. . . I wanted to tell you straight away but Ben said. . . I'm sorry, sorry, sorry. I never meant to hurt your feelings. . . I hope that, later on, we can be friends. . . Yours, Sara*

The doorbell rang. I took a deep breath, a feeling of great annoyance brewing up in me. Screwing the letter up and chucking it on the floor, I pulled open the front door ready to tell Tina Hicks to get lost.

"Hi, Julia. That was quick!"

My cousin, Kath, walked in, a giant smile on her face, her cheeks red from the cold. She struggled out of a heavy coat and scarf to show her nurse's dress underneath.

"Chop chop. A cup of tea would go down well," she said, in her usual bossy way.

I groaned inwardly. The only two people I had to talk to. Saint Kath or Tina Hicks. What a choice.

Bobby stayed in the Special Baby Unit until the doctors were sure that he was physically fit. His weight was good and he was able to feed without any trouble. The nurses said he'd been well cared for.

The police wanted to find his mother. They issued statements to the press: *police officers are keen to speak to the mother of the child; the child's mother may well be in need of medical attention; the mother could come forward at any time without fear of prosecution.* There was no response to these pleas. The police put them out on local radio and news programmes. Then they went to the national press. It was always possible, they thought, that the baby had been driven there from some other place. Their traffic division was looking closely at CCTV footage of the nearby roads in the hours leading up to the discovery.

PC Robert Mathews visited the hospital. A film crew shot footage of him sitting with the tiny boy on his lap. A voice-over was used. *The abandoned baby, Bobby, is pictured here with the police officer who found him. Police are very keen for the boy's mother to contact them. Bobby is a sweet and good-natured baby and he needs his mother. The police are sure that Bobby's mother needs him. They are urging Bobby's mother to contact them. . .*

But there was no contact. No word at all from the baby's mother. PC Mathews (Robbie, his mates called him) couldn't understand it. In his bag he'd brought a tiny babygro in the colours of Manchester United, his football team.

How could anyone leave something so helpless in a cardboard box?

CHAPTER THREE

A couple of weeks later, at lunchtime, I was sitting alone in my form room flicking through a magazine when Sara and Ben Holland burst in. They were both laughing at something and stopped suddenly when they saw me. It was embarrassing. I'd got tired of wandering around school, trying to avoid my old friends, making myself look as inconspicuous as I could. I'd wanted some privacy.

So had they.

"Oh!" Sara said, stopping in her tracks.

The smile dropped off Ben's face when he saw me sitting in the corner.

"Julia," he said and patted his pocket, automatically feeling for his mobile.

It was a habit of his. When he was in awkward situations he reverted to his mobile, looking at the screen for messages or listening for a ring tone. *I thought I heard it ring*, he'd say, the moment passing, his discomfort over. He'd done it that first time we'd been in his bedroom, standing up, away from the bed, pulling his clothes together. The memory of it unsettled me.

"We were just looking for. . ." Sara started.

Ben mumbled the names of his mates. I knew them, had hung around with them. Now they seemed like strangers.

"Let's go. . ." Ben said, tersely.

"See you. . ." Sara said.

And they were gone, their footsteps sounding along the corridor, crisp at first but then melting into the mass of distant sounds from fifteen hundred scattered kids on a lunch break.

I breathed out, feeling my heart beating slowly and steadily. It hadn't happened much; me coming face to face with them. It was to be expected when we were moving around the same building, involved with the same teachers and groups of friends. Up to that point there had always been other people around and I'd been able to ignore their presence, to pretend they were nothing, just faces in the crowd, two kids who I'd once known. I usually walked around with my eyes forward, stepping purposefully as though I had an appointment with someone and was already late for it.

It was how I got through my day.

As soon as the bell for the end of school went I walked to the toilets by the science blocks. The area was deserted and I could only hear the noise of departing pupils from a distance. I went into the loos and looked in the mirror. My hair looked brown rather than fair, and my eyelids heavy, as though I was about to drop off for a nap. It was hard work keeping up face, trying to pretend that I didn't care. It was preferable to hide in the toilets rather than push my way through the throng at the school gates. I wanted to avoid the reunion of the young lovers after they'd been so cruelly parted by their A-level classes. From somewhere outside I heard footsteps and female voices. With no time to slip out I went into the farthest stall and closed the door.

I recognized the voices when they came in. It was Tricia and Lou from one of my groups. I sat down on the toilet and groaned inwardly. The two girls hardly drew breath, they were talking so quickly. The smell of tobacco smoke wafted in. They were talking about someone's cousin who was getting married the following Saturday, then they moved on to the cost of weddings in general and the pros and cons of spending so much in one day.

What made them think of me and Ben Holland I just couldn't say. After a gap of seconds, where I imagined one or other of them inhaling from a cigarette, Lou started to speak.

"Did you see Sara Dewey with Ben Holland?"

"That's old news. That was weeks ago."

"I *know*," Lou said, raising her voice in an indignant way. "I've known for ages. I'm just saying. He always has a girl hanging round him."

I was listening intently, every bit of my body still.

"Julia Diamond looks crap these days."

"I'm surprised he stayed with her so long."

"Don't say that! She's nice, Julia. She's a laugh," Tricia said.

"Yeah, well she's got everyone laughing at her now."

"It's not her fault he dumped her. If you ask me it's that Sara. She was supposed to be her best friend. If I had a friend like that I'd. . ."

"I heard he only went out with her for one thing."

"One thing? You mean sex?"

"No, dope. Her stamp collection!"

"So what? Julia's not a nun, is she?"

"Yeah, but it turns out that she jumped into his bed as soon as she got off with him."

"His *bed*?"

Tricia's voice had lowered. She sounded incredulous. I closed my eyes not wanting to hear any more.

"Not his *bed* as such. Well, it might have been his bed, I don't know. Point is she went all the way with him straight away. Once you let them do what they want they don't want you any more."

Their voices moved away and then I heard the sound of the outside door creaking open.

"You sound like my mum!" Tricia said.

"It's true. You don't give it all away at once. . ."

They left and I sat there for a long time. Ben had told someone. Of course he had. He'd said he wouldn't. *It's between us, you and me*, he'd whispered in my ear and I had thought he meant it. Me? I hadn't said a word to anyone. Not even Sara. Especially not Sara. Now she knew and all the kids knew. *Julia Diamond had sex with Ben Holland on the day after the Christmas party.*

I couldn't deny it because it was true.

CHAPTER FOUR

I found a Post-it stuck to the hall mirror when I got in.

I'm in Marilyn's. You can make a start on the tea. Spag Bol. Jar of sauce in the cupboard. Luv Mum XXXX

I sighed. My mum was making a habit of being over at Marilyn Hicks's house. I put my bag down at the bottom of the stairs and hung my coat over the banister. I felt miffed. Marilyn was probably giving my mum her whole life story *again*. I went through to the kitchen and filled up the kettle. I opened the fridge door and got the tea things out. A plastic tray of minced meat. Spaghetti Bolognese. The thought of it made me feel a bit queasy. Whether that was the food or hearing horrible gossip about myself I wasn't sure. Where was my mum when I needed her? I got the chopping board out and the onions and mushrooms and started to prepare the meal.

OK, I did have sex with Ben Holland the day after the Christmas disco. It wasn't quite as calculated as Lou made it sound, though. I hadn't planned for it to happen and I hadn't felt particularly marvellous afterwards.

It was Saturday and Ben and I had arranged to meet outside McDonald's just after lunch. I'd got up early and bathed, washed my hair and generally spent the morning walking round looking at myself in the mirror. I was wearing new clothes that had been bought for Christmas. A pink jumper that zipped up the front and a long black skirt with a side split. My boots were polished and I'd put nail varnish on. I thought we would go to the park but when we met he said that his family were out Christmas shopping and that we could go to his house to relax. I went along. I was still bubbling from the previous night and I would probably have gone to China with him if he'd asked me. He took me straight to his bedroom.

"I'll show you my computer," he said, even though I hadn't asked to look at it.

I followed him. I wasn't stupid. I had a good idea of the things we would do when we got up there. When he closed his bedroom door and gave me kiss after kiss on the mouth I felt my legs trembling and my chest aching. Behind him was a double bed that looked as though it had been hastily made up. The rest of his room was more untidy. There were clothes hanging over the wardrobe door and on the back of his desk chair. The computer was on, its screensaver building impossible shapes in garish colours. Across his desk were half-filled glasses of orange squash. I wanted to laugh. *Who drinks orange squash?* I thought.

After a few minutes he pulled back.

"Let's get comfortable," he whispered and nodded towards the bed.

He wrestled with the duvet, making it smoother, and I sat down on it feeling a whoosh of air. I crossed my legs neatly, the split of my skirt allowing one leg to stick out. My boots felt heavy.

"Why don't you take those off?" he said.

I unzipped them and threw them to the side. I pulled my legs up on to the bed and tucked them underneath. He lay back against the pillows and I lay against him playing with the zipper on my cardigan. Then he started to speak.

"The first time I noticed you, you were wearing your waitress uniform."

"I don't remember!" I said. "When was that?"

"My family were having a meal at the Willow Tree. I saw you walking round and I thought you looked familiar. You kept scratching your head with your pen. Then I remembered you were the Diamond kid in year twelve."

"I'm not a kid!" I said, giving him a light smack, pretending to be annoyed. I liked the nickname though. *The Diamond Kid.*

"I know that," he said, his hand reaching to my face and pulling me towards him.

Those first few kisses on the bed were a blur. My mind was elsewhere. I was in the restaurant, walking round, taking orders, feeling grown-up. All the while he was there without me knowing. Ben Holland. A boy that I'd fancied from afar, a boy who I never thought I had a chance with. He was watching me, weighing me up, trying to place me. He admired me from a distance and I never even knew it was happening. It gave me this heady feeling and this burst of energy and I reached for him and kissed him hungrily.

"You're lovely," he whispered, taking a breath and then leaning across me, his hand fluttering on to my breast.

My head felt light and I was hardly breathing as his fingers pulled down the zip of my jumper. I lay back on the bed and he moved one of his legs until it was in between mine. I put my hand in his hair and pulled it gently. I could hear his breaths, deep and long as his fingers slipped into the split of my skirt. All the while I had this picture in my head of me in my blue uniform, writing down the food orders and Ben looking at me across the room, recognizing me, wanting me. It made me feel exhilarated, every inch of my skin tingling with anticipation.

The black skirt. It had been bought to be worn on Christmas day. It was something Mum liked. Both of us usually had new Christmas day outfits. *It makes it more special*, my mum always said.

I wondered afterwards whether things would have been different if I'd been wearing trousers. Taking moments to stand up, off the bed; to undo the button and the zip, take them off one leg at a time. Would that have given me a moment's cooling-off time? A few seconds to think, to pull back, to say *Hang on a minute, this is too much, too soon.*

The skirt slid up. It was that easy. Somehow he was on top of me. It wasn't rushed and he didn't put any pressure on me.

"Are you all right?" he whispered.

My eyes were closed but I could tell that he was doing something, fiddling with his trousers, moving clothes around, fixing the duvet which had become tangled up beneath us.

"Sure you're OK?" he said, his voice croaking.

And I was. I was in a kind of daze that I couldn't pull back from. My whole body was thrilled with every touch and in my head I was just grinning to myself. It wasn't that I had pined after him. He had seen me in the restaurant and *wanted* me. I lay back transported. Had anything this brilliant ever happened to me? It was over in seconds and he lay there for a minute before rolling away. Holding on to his clothes he stood up, off the bed.

"Is that my ring tone?" he said, reaching for his mobile phone.

I sat up and straightened my clothes. The skirt was creased and I noticed that the stitching had pulled apart at the split. It depressed me suddenly. *I won't be able to wear it on Christmas Day*, I thought. I zipped up my pink jumper and felt a dull sensation of worry. Ben turned back and gave me a grin.

"Did you use something?" I said, coughing slightly, thinking of all the lessons we had had about contraception.

"Course I did," he said, looking away from me, using his thumb to send a message on his mobile.

The sound of the front door opening broke into my thoughts. I sat up straight, looked over at the mince and onions waiting to be cooked. I heard my mum's voice singing out.

"Julia!"

"Here," I called.

I felt a ripple of relief. I didn't want to be on my own any more. I didn't want to have to play over Tricia and Lou's words in my mind. *He only wanted her for one thing.*

The kitchen door opened and my mum came in.

"Sorry, I'm late. I've been with Marilyn. . ."

"I *know*," I said.

"Poor Marilyn. . ."

My mum was rubbing her hands together, her forehead crinkled up. She looked as if she was going to launch into some sympathetic analysis of Tina's mum's sad life. I wasn't in the mood for it.

"I don't want to hear about Marilyn Hicks," I said, in a sharper tone than I intended.

"Oh."

My mum nodded, her lips all pursed up. I knew that expression. It was the *OK, I know you're not interested in anyone else's life*.

"What I mean is, I've not had a brilliant day myself."

"It's absolutely fine, don't worry," she said, in a clipped voice, slicing her words off one by one.

She was still wearing her smart restaurant clothes; dark suit, white shirt, plain leather shoes. On her lapel was a badge that said *Gill Diamond, Dining Room Manager*.

"I'll just pop upstairs to get changed," she said, bouncing out of the room before I could say another word.

CHAPTER

I listened to my mum's footsteps receding upstairs. Her bedroom door closed sharply and then there was quiet. I'd been an idiot. I'd taken my bad mood out on her when she was only trying to be nice to a neighbour. I pictured Marilyn Hicks with her heavy make-up and tight clothes. I remembered her husband, Ray, the computer nerd, always in a brightly coloured shirt as though he had just returned from a holiday in Hawaii. He used to surf, someone said. They had been the odd couple.

I busied myself with the food, washing up as I went along, keen to make it up to my mum. After a while she came down wearing jeans and a sweatshirt and a huge pair of fluffy slippers.

"This looks good," she said, cheerfully, looking at the pan. She never stayed in a bad mood for long.

I drained the pasta and put it on two plates. "Sorry, Mum," I said.

She shrugged her shoulders and sat down at the

table. I poured the meat sauce on to the pasta and set her plate in front of her. She used her fork to mix it up, blowing at the steam that was rising off it. Then she twisted some up on a spoon and put it into her mouth, making an *umm* noise. I played around with mine.

"What's up with Marilyn Hicks?" I said.

"Thought you weren't interested."

I shrugged my shoulders.

"She's depressed."

"She's always depressed. What is it now?"

"She's upset about Ray leaving."

"That was months ago. Six months ago."

"No," my mum shook her head. "It was just before Christmas."

She was right. I remembered the van parked outside their house. It was a cold day and Ray Hicks had a long check overcoat on that reached down to his ankles and swayed like a cloak when he walked. At his neck I could see a flash of orange from his shirt. Marilyn was standing on the pavement in a blouse and skirt, the breeze making the fabric ripple. She had her arms crossed, hugging herself against the cold.

"She can't seem to get over him. It's Ray this and Ray that and she wants to get back together with him for a trial period. One day he agrees and the next day he changes his mind. That's what she says, anyway."

"Didn't you say she was a bit dippy?" I said, pointing my finger at the side of my head.

"I said she suffered from depression. She's on tablets. I never said she was *dippy*, as you put it!"

"Sorry."

"It's a proper illness. She has prescription drugs for it."

"I know!" I said.

My mum sighed. "You must promise me you will never say a word of this to Tina."

"I promise. It's not like I even talk to Tina that much!"

"Yes, well. That's another sad story," she said, giving me a sour look.

I forked up some food and chewed rigorously. I was not going to get into another *Why don't you try to be friends with Tina* conversation.

"He's not Tina's dad, is he?" I said.

"No, Marilyn and Ray were only married for four years. They've been having problems for a while. They moved here to make a fresh start. You know, new house, spending time together. It didn't work out."

"Where's he gone?"

"He's in a flat nearby. That's part of the problem. She keeps going round to see him. Turning up at different times of the day and night. She thinks she can make him fall in love with her again. It's so sad."

I pictured Ray Hicks looking round the edge of his curtains and seeing Marilyn knocking on his front door. I imagined him rolling his eyes.

"Wasn't he younger than her?"

"Five years younger. It's one of the things that upsets Marilyn. She says he's going to find some thirty-year-old."

"He's no oil painting," I said.

My mum gave me a look of irritation. An *end of her tether* look.

"Well, none of us are," she said, and added, "And you of all people should have some sympathy for Marilyn. You know what it feels like to be rejected."

"It's not the same!" I said.

"No, you're right. It's not the same. It's ten times worse for Marilyn. She's thirty-nine with no money, no job, no career, no social life. On top of it all she suffers from depression."

She stopped eating and pushed her plate away, finally exasperated with me.

"Sorry, I'm not as hungry as I thought I was. Most probably my period's coming. I'll just go upstairs and have a shower. That'll perk me up."

I listened to her footsteps going up the stairs for the second time in an hour. Why was I so testy with her? Would it have hurt me to give Tina's mum a bit of sympathy? Maybe my period was due as well. Maybe that's why I was finding it so hard to cheer up.

I cleared the food away, leaving the leftovers in a dish in the fridge. When I was finished I found myself thinking about my period. I looked across the room at the wall calendar. I had been expecting to start for a while. I wasn't exactly regular but the last period seemed an age ago. I took the calendar off the wall and flicked back to the previous month. January 9th was ringed. It was a Thursday and the pains had started late in the afternoon, I remembered. I counted through the weeks. Almost nine Thursdays had passed. Eight weeks. I was irregular, I knew that, had been ever since I'd started. Sometimes it was four weeks between periods but just as often it was five or six, and once I'd missed a period completely.

I sat down at the table. Further down the page, Saturday 28th January was also ringed. Beside it my mum had written *Julia out with Hollands*. A day out with Ben's family. I'd been so thrilled to be asked that I was up and ready hours before they were due to collect me. I watched out of my mum's bedroom window for every car that came along the street. I kept counting. *It'll be the sixth car from now on* I said to myself. Actually it had been the tenth. I had skipped down the stairs and pulled the front door open before Ben had even had a chance to knock on it.

From upstairs I could hear the toilet flushing and my mum moving around. I'd been horrible to her ever since she came home. I opened the drawer and got out a pad of fluorescent pink Post-its and wrote a note.

Sorry for being a complete ratbag. Luv Julia XXXX

I put the calendar back on the wall and went out into the hall and stuck the Post-it on the mirror.

Eight weeks between periods. It was normal for me. There was no need to worry anyway, because Ben always took care. He told me that, reassured me.

He always used a condom.

Except for that one time, when we went to Suffolk with his family and went off for a walk by ourselves. Then there was no condom to use.

Bobby was leaving hospital. The nurses were sorry to see him go. His social worker, Beverly, had been shopping and bought him everything new: six babygros, vests and bootees; fleecy jackets and padded trousers. Tiny gloves that he had to wear to stop him scratching his own skin. A packet of three stretchy hats to keep his head warm: red, white and blue. They looked like boiled egg warmers.

The police kept all the clothes that Bobby had been wearing when he was found. They also kept the covers and the pet carrier. These things might be clues, they said. They might point in the direction of the mother, they said.

Beverly was a tall black lady with heavy gold glasses and straightened hair that shone like coal. Her earrings hung to her jaw line and when she turned her head they swung back and forth for moments afterwards. Whenever she came to the hospital she made a point of sitting by Bobby's cot and talking to him.

"You and me? We're going to meet some nice people who will look after you until we find your mummy," she said, using her fingers to pull at her hair and pat it neatly into the curve of her neck.

"They have a lovely cot for you and they have other children who cannot wait until you get there."

While she was there Robert Mathews came. He was in his uniform and stood on the other side of the cot. They looked like two giants peering over the tiny boy.

"How are you, lad? Are they treating you all right?" the policeman said using a high-pitched baby voice.

Beverly laughed out loud and reached across and gave the policeman a playful shove.

"Now Mr Mathews. You can speak to Bobby in a normal voice. Unless of course that is your normal voice?"

"Oh, call me Robbie," he said, turning away to cough into his hand.

The police had a lot of CCTV footage to check. The doctor's surgery was on a corner across the road from a garage and a church. Both had security cameras. Further down the road was a major set of traffic lights and beyond that a roundabout. After a thorough search they came up with something important. They called a press conference and showed the moving footage to a dozen or so reporters.

"See here," Frank Sullivan, the detective in charge of the case, said. He was pointing at a giant television screen with a pen. "At five forty-five am. we have two cars waiting to go on to Junction Roundabout. The second one, which you can just see pulling up, is a pale-coloured car, some kind of hatchback. Now if we move forward to five forty-seven, the pale car is the first at the traffic lights. It sits for a moment and then you can see – and this is important. . ."

The detective froze the picture as a lorry drove up beside the car.

"A builder's lorry, quite distinctive, drives up beside the hatchback. It has ladders and planks and along the side the name of the company in italics. Too difficult for us to read, although our labs are trying to enlarge the image."

He cleared his throat and looked straight towards the cameras.

"Whoever was driving that lorry may have glanced to the side and seen the hatchback and the people in it. They may, without knowing, have important information. Now. . ."

He turned back and the film jumped forward.

"This is the CCTV footage from the garage. You'll see, in the top left-hand corner the street outside. At five forty-nine a pale car pulls up. After a few seconds someone gets out of the passenger side. You can't see much of them because the image is too far away. This person pauses for a moment and then opens the back of the car and takes something out. The pet carrier, we believe."

The inspector paused for effect.

"The person, who we believe is a woman, moves out of the shot and takes the baby in the box over to the doctor's surgery. Now they come back into shot, get back into the car. The car moves off out of shot."

"Is that it?" one of the reporters called.

"No, one more thing. This last footage is from the church camera. It doesn't actually overlook the surgery or the place where the car was parked. It does overlook the street just round the corner. See, now the time is six-ten. The pale car is parked just round the corner from the surgery. Now you see the passenger door opening. This time we get a much better look at the person. You can see by the shape that it's female although she is wearing a hooded top which covers most of her face. She's wearing jeans, and notice the heeled shoes. She walks towards the corner and then seems to stand there for a few moments. Then she turns quickly and runs towards the car. Only seconds later the car revs up and drives out of shot. She was waiting, you see. Waiting for someone to come and find the baby. At six-ten the baby was found by a passing policeman, as you all know."

There was a murmur of conversation and the rustle of people moving about. The detective patted the television set proudly, pleased with the conference.

Beverly carried Bobby out to her car. She had the baby carrier over her arm like a shopping basket. Over her other shoulder was a bag with all Bobby's things in it. One of the nurses came along, opening doors so that she could get through. Fixing the seatbelt around the carrier she stood up, a little breathless from the walk, her earrings swinging like pendulums. She patted her hair and walked round to the driver's seat.

"Come on, Bobby," she said, as she got into the car. "Let's take you home."

CHAPTER SIX

Ben Holland and me spent a lot of time together but we didn't have sex all the time. In school I wanted to stop Lou and Tricia and put them straight. I didn't though. I sat in a desk at the back of the classroom with my head buried in a magazine. Whenever I heard new people coming into the room I raised my eyes to see who it was. Tricia came in on her own and didn't even glance in my direction. Lou came a few moments later, talking to a couple of boys. Moments later Sara came in, looking breathless, as if she'd run all the way down the corridor. I knew that look. Waiting on the footbridge with Ben until the very last minute. Just a few more snatched kisses, a bear hug, my chest pushed hard against his. It used to make me dizzy. When the time came we both ran up to the school gates. It was a wrench to split off from him and go to my classes.

Sara sat down at a desk near the front. She looked at the kids immediately around her but avoided turning to my part of the classroom. I stared at the back of her jacket for a few minutes wondering if she could feel my eyes there, heavy with reproach.

Later, in History, I felt a bit better. There was almost no one in the class that I knew very well. I got my coursework out as the teacher came into the room. A long essay about the Second World War. Most of the kids in the class were on their final drafts. Me? I was still trying to put together my first attempt.

I can't say my schoolwork had suffered during the weeks that I was with Ben. If anything it was the opposite. Ben Holland spent hours on his work. That's why he didn't have a part-time job. His mum and dad gave him pots of money just so that he would study. He was top student. He influenced me and for a while I tried to keep up with homework. Sara, on the other hand, had always been more than just an average student. She had a room full of books for a start, and a desk with a computer on it. Her assignments were always neatly typed out with bold headings and underlinings. She cared about her work. How much better it would be for Ben to have a girlfriend like that. How well they fitted together.

What had he ever seen in me?

I sensed a rustling from the next seat. Tina Hicks was sitting there sorting through her rucksack producing notebooks and plastic folders and library textbooks. When she saw I was looking she gave me a tentative smile. I nodded briskly at her. The teacher was fiddling with an OHP and there was the murmur of quiet chatter coming from the rest of the class.

"I'm late," Tina said in a loud whisper. "My mum."

She didn't explain and I didn't ask.

"You all right?" she said.

"Fine," I said.

She was tidying her desktop squaring her books up to the corners. I noticed her coursework essay sitting on top of everything. It had been typed on a computer and the title was in bold. It looked so incredibly neat and organized and *impressive*. My own rough notes looked childish and pathetic beside it. For a moment I wanted to screw them up into a ball and chuck them away.

"I wondered if you would do me a favour," Tina said.

I looked up from my assignment.

"My mum says your cousin's a nurse?"

I nodded, my mouth pursing slightly at the mention of Saint Kath.

"I thought I might have a chat with her? Only I'm thinking of going into nursing."

I made a face.

She flinched at this and my jaw clenched. Why was I always so *offhand* with her.

"Sorry! Thing is I don't get on that well with my cousin. She's a bit of a holier than thou type, you know. . ."

Sara and I used to laugh at Kath. Sara called her a nun and said that she was the sort of person who probably wore huge white knickers and a vest.

"Oh."

"But you can definitely chat to her. This is her second year in nursing and I'm sure she'll tell you whatever you need to know. She comes to tea every week. I'll tell you when then you can join us. Mum won't mind."

A rapping sound came from the front of the room. The teacher had fixed up the OHP and wanted everyone's attention. I sat up, pretending to take notice. Inside I was groaning. I'd actually invited Tina around to my house for tea. My mum would smile and think that we were becoming friends. I'd lost everything, my boyfriend and my best friend, and I was being driven towards Tina Hicks. At the end of the lesson I stood up, sweeping all my bits of paper into my bag, and left the room before Tina had even shut her books. I wanted her to be absolutely clear that just because I'd said she could come and talk to my cousin it didn't mean we were going to hang around together.

I left school the moment the bell went and managed to get out of the gates before most kids had got out of their classroom doors. I walked quickly along over the footbridge and noticed, with surprise, a heaviness in my belly and the tops of my legs. Maybe even, I thought, a hint of pain. It must be a sign; any moment I would feel the cramping sensation that would make me want to lie down and wrap myself up in my duvet. My period.

At last.

I got the tampons out and the painkillers from the medicine cupboard. I checked all evening, running up to the toilet every half hour or so. Each time I expected to see a splash of red. Something I usually dreaded. Five days when I felt washed out and extra ratty. Five days of discomfort and disposing of tampons, changing my underwear three times a day. This time I was ready and waiting. This time I welcomed it, I *longed* for it.

But nothing happened, so I went to bed.

On Wednesday, Tina Hicks came round for tea to meet Kath. She had dressed up as though she was going out for the evening. She had dark trousers on and a loose top and didn't look nearly as heavy as she did in her school clothes. Her hair was loose too, and was thicker and longer than I had thought.

Kath came late, bringing in a blast of cold air as she bustled into the kitchen. Her cheeks were scarlet and her nose like a red button. She wasn't wearing her nurse's uniform because she'd finished work at lunchtime and had been home to change.

"I'm starving," she said.

This was usual. Kath had a big appetite. She loved her food and was always talking about things that she'd made or was going to make or meals she'd eaten in restaurants. She didn't seem to mind that she was on the big side.

"I'm a proper-sized woman," she'd say, "not one of those skeletons you see in the magazines. What man wants to get into bed with someone like that?"

She liked to be rude as well, thinking she was shocking us. She was always telling me and mum about the sights she'd seen in the hospital; bottoms and bosoms and willies.

"This is Tina, one of our neighbours," my mum said, when Kath had got her coat off and sat down. "She wants to be a nurse!"

Tina went coy and I was sure that she was blushing.

"Brilliant," Kath said.

She was always saying stuff like that. *Super. Excellent. Terrific.* Her enthusiasm could wear anyone down.

My mum was fussing at the oven and Kath was fiddling with her knife and fork as if she just couldn't wait. The smell of garlic was strong and it made me feel queasy for a moment.

"After my A levels I want to work with people with mental health problems. . ." Tina said, in a tiny voice, glancing at me nervously.

"That's a really good area to get into. It's not that popular, either. Most people who go into nursing want to work with children. Not many people want to spend their days with difficult, damaged people. Is that lasagne?"

"Julia made it."

I made a little bow as though I was being applauded.

"You still have to study all the core stuff: adult, paediatrics, geriatrics. It's only later that you specialize. I've just finished a stint on the maternity wing. Oh, just a scoop of salad for me," Kath said. "I'll tell you one thing. I don't think I'll ever have a baby. Not after what I've seen over the last six weeks!"

I looked at the plate in front of me. A steaming mass of colours, yellow, brown, red, green. I pushed my fork into it but didn't eat.

"Tina's got some experience of illness. You don't mind me saying, do you, Tina? Her mum has suffered from depression for years."

"That's a shame. But there's lots they can do to help nowadays."

"I know. Mum has medication."

"Umm. . . This is good, Julia."

"Don't sound so shocked!" I said, taking a tiny forkful.

"Maybe you could have a career as a cook! They're always looking for people in McDonald's."

"Oh ha ha. . ."

By the time the meal was over I was feeling exhausted listening to my cousin telling Tina about her entire career in the NHS, so I washed up and told them to go and chat for a while in the living room. My mum came out after a few minutes.

"That was lovely. Tina's a really bright girl. I can see why Marilyn leans on her so much."

"Um. . ."

I was suddenly feeling really tired. There was also the hint of pain in the bottom of my stomach.

"You look a bit under the weather," my mum said. "Is it your period?"

I nodded. I wasn't sure but it felt like it. I finished washing up and went upstairs to the bathroom. After Kath and Tina had gone I popped in and out of the toilet all evening.

Nothing. No sign of my period. So I went to bed.

CHAPTER SEVEN

A few days later I found myself in the chemist's superstore on the trading estate a couple of bus stops past school. It had been almost twelve weeks since I'd had a period and I wasn't feeling that good. My mum thought I looked run-down and had suggested a visit to the doctor's. I was crying at the drop of a hat, and when I stood sideways and looked into the mirror I could see my stomach sticking out, stretching my skirt or jeans to the limit.

What to do if I was actually pregnant.

It was a question I'd left unanswered for days, weeks even. It had been there filed at the back of my worries, a kind of mental Post-it. There were two options. To have a baby or have an abortion. It was as bald as that. No halfway, no shades of this or shades of that. Both options made me feel light-headed, mildly ill. Neither was better than the other. If I had the baby everyone would know and would feel pity for me. I'd be seen as an idiot. *Fancy getting pregnant in this day and age! Like, hasn't she heard of contraception?* Others would think it served me right. *Well, if she will go round having sex on the first night what can she expect?* Sara and Ben would know. *It's not just your fault,* Sara would probably say to Ben. *It takes two to make a baby.* Ben would think that I'd done it on purpose, that I was trying to hold on to him.

Then there was the actual baby to think about.

I pictured myself as a young mum, walking behind a pushchair trying to ignore some wailing toddler, wearing last year's fashions, overweight and tired. I'd seen girls like that in clothes shops, looking enviously at sparkly tops and tight skirts, high heels and long boots. All the time their kid was twisting and turning, pulling at the racks of garments, whining about wanting this or that. I did not want to be like that.

But an *abortion*.

The very word made my stomach heavy and my feet feel like lead.

Suffolk with Ben's family had been freezing. It was the end of January so we should have expected it. The area was flat and we could see for miles. Ben's dad had binoculars and handed them around for everyone to have a better look. Even though we weren't at the seafront we could feel the cold wind

49

from the North Sea and almost taste the salt in the air. I had a warm jacket and fleece and Ben was wearing a long heavy coat, but we were both chilled to the bone. His mum and dad were striding ahead and Ben and me went for a walk in the woods. The moment we lost sight of his parents he rounded on me pressing me up against a tree, kissing me as though he hadn't seen me for months, his mouth hot, his breath searing on my cold face.

"Don't," I'd said, when he tried to unzip my jacket.

"Just to keep my hand warm," he'd whispered.

I'd given in, the feel of his hand on my warm breast making my knees buckle. After a while we'd walked further into the wood out of the raw wind and found some soft ground. I lay down and he lay beside me, his long coat covering my legs. After a few minutes of kissing he took the coat off.

"You'll freeze," I whispered.

"This is to keep you warm," he said, tugging at the zip on my jeans.

I arched my back while he pulled my boots and jeans off, and then lay on them. He covered me up and then used his coat like a duvet. I lay back and felt my blood pulsing through me. I was no longer cold. I was no longer aware of where we were. I was focusing on Ben, the weight of his body, his face in my neck and his tight grip. I was in a kind of daze, not thinking about anything, just feeling him moving back and forward, his hair tickling my skin.

When it was over he lay very still for a minute. Then he raised himself up.

"Are you OK?" he said, smiling.

I nodded. I was always OK with him.

"Don't worry," he said. "I pulled back."

I nodded even though I had no idea what he was talking about. It was only later, much later that he told me he hadn't used a condom. At the time I didn't care. When I was with him I didn't care about anything.

How could we have been so stupid?

I walked through the doors of the huge chemist's store. How much did a pregnancy test cost? I had about twelve pounds in my purse, and my cash card. I headed for a neon sign in the far corner that said *Pharmacy*. I lowered my head and walked through the aisles of face creams, make-up and vitamins. I found what I wanted immediately, stacked up next to women's sanitary products. There were two to choose from. I picked up a blue packet that had the words *Expectations – Pregnancy Testing Kit*. It was the size of a packet of toothpaste. I paused for a minute and held it sideways to read the instructions. It was a simple urine test. If the applicator showed a blue line then it was positive. The word *positive* made me wrinkle my brow. I tapped my fingers on the box and then walked towards the counter, my hand in my bag trying to locate my purse. The assistant was standing ready for me. She was a woman of my mum's age and had a white jacket on, as if she wasn't just any shop worker but someone who was in charge of important drugs. She had black square glasses on that made her look a bit like a doctor.

I handed the box to her, avoiding eye contact, and placed two five-pound notes on a shelf by the till. She never flinched, she simply scanned the box and then put it into a plastic bag. I held my hand out waiting for my change, wishing she would hurry up so that I could get out and go home. When she finally counted out the coins I turned away and began to stuff the money into my purse. I was all fingers and thumbs though, and the plastic bag slipped out of my grasp and fell, the box spilling out and lying on the ground like headline news:

Expectations – Pregnancy Testing Kit

I squatted down to retrieve it but someone had got there first and was picking it up and handing it to me.

"Hi, Julia."

It was Tina Hicks and she was holding my pregnancy test.

I couldn't answer for a moment. I was full of indignation. What the hell was she doing there?

"Is this for you?" she said, reading the brand name back and forth.

She was wearing casual clothes, jeans and a short leather jacket that I hadn't seen before. Instead of her mammoth rucksack she had a small one with a tiny teddy bear hanging from it.

"What are you doing here?" I demanded, snatching the pregnancy test from her hand.

"I'm getting a prescription. . ." she said, pointing towards the pharmacy.

"Oh," I said, deflated, the pregnancy test sitting in my hand for all to see. I shoved it back into its bag. "Oh, sorry, I. . ."

"I won't be a minute," she said. "Then I'm walking back. I'll keep you company, if you like."

She turned and walked towards the pharmacy counter and I heard her asking to see the pharmacist. I was left standing on my own. Without another look at her I marched towards the exit, pushing hard against the swing doors. Once outside I felt utterly stupid. What was wrong with me? Every time I set eyes on Tina Hicks I found myself being rude. She was friendly and nice but she was second best to me and every time I was with her I was reminded of my proper friend, Sara. It was like losing a ten-pound note and finding a couple of pound coins. It was a horrible thing to say but I felt short-changed.

I stopped outside the shop and sat on a bollard. The cold wind ruffled my clothes but I didn't move. After a few moments I saw her walking towards the doors, heading in my direction. She had what looked like a carrier bag full of drugs for her depressed mum. When she caught sight of me she smiled.

"The local drug dealer, that's me," she said, holding up a plastic bag full of bottles and boxes. "We could wait for a bus, but I don't mind walking if you don't," she said.

"Why do you come all the way over here?" I said, getting into step beside her. "There must be chemists' shops that are closer."

"My mum doesn't like me to go local. She thinks people might talk. Anyway, the walk does me good."

We continued along the road, leaving the trading park behind, passing some open ground and playing fields. I remembered, with a heavy feeling, the package I had in my hand and what I had to do with it. I also remembered that Tina had seen it as clear as day.

"That thing I dropped," I said, quickening my steps to keep up with her. "It's not what it seems."

"You mean it's not a pregnancy testing kit?"

"Well, it is. Yes, it is. But it's not for me."

She didn't say anything. Coming towards us, on the pavement, were two boys on bikes. We each stepped aside to let them past.

"Your cousin's nice," Tina said.

"Um. . ." I said.

"She's getting me some brochures about courses. . ."

She went quiet. I opened my mouth to speak but nothing came out. We both seemed to be walking in step, she just a little faster than me so that I had to keep up.

"That test kit," I finally said. "It is for me."

"Oh," she said.

A bus pulled up, on the other side of the road, its brakes screeching. The doors opened and a single woman got off. She looked up at the sky and immediately put up an umbrella. I glanced up. There wasn't a cloud in sight.

"I don't think I'm *actually* pregnant. I'm just a bit late. That's all."

She nodded and drew a quick deep breath.

"Actually I'm quite a lot late. It's happened before. But this time."

"You're probably still irregular," she said. "I know I am."

It was what I wanted to hear.

"I go months between periods."

"I can, too," I said. "But this time. With Ben, you know we. . . You've probably heard anyway. Everyone's talking about it."

"Heard about what?"

"People are saying. You know. That he only went out with me for one thing."

"I heard that. It's rubbish. I saw you two together a load of times. He seemed really fond of you."

A van ambled past. *He seemed really fond of you.* These words had an extraordinary effect on me. I straightened my shoulders. I ran my fingers through my hair and took a deep breath pushing my chest out. An odd feeling was forming inside my chest. Pride. I felt a rush inside. He had been fond of me. *He had.*

"Thing is, if you think about it, it might make Sara feel a bit easier about what she did. If the story goes round that he didn't really care about you then it doesn't seem so bad that she took him. I know she's your friend and stuff, and I don't want to take any sides, but. . ."

I looked at her with gratitude. She looked terribly innocent with her teddy bear hanging off her bag.

"I did have sex with him."

"I'm not saying you didn't. But it wasn't just a one-night thing. You were with him for a while?"

I was. I looked down at the pavement, a sudden feeling of sadness welling up inside me. Ten weeks, and he'd liked me, I knew he had.

We came up to the school. The gates were closed and locked and the buildings behind deserted. The place had bad associations for me now and only made me feel gloomy. A motorbike buzzed past and I heard a heavy sound, like lorries in the distance.

"It's not nice breaking up with someone," Tina said. "I know. It's happened to me."

"Really?"

"A while ago, and I don't think I was as cut up about it as you are. But it still hurts."

"At least he didn't go off with your best friend!" I said.

"Ah. But maybe you've got to ask yourself, was she ever really your best friend? If she was prepared to do that?"

It made me think. *My best friend*. Was she really that?

We had left the school behind and were walking across the footbridge. I stopped halfway and leaned on the railing. On one side of the road were the grounds of the golf club and further back the school and its playing fields. On the other side were rows of streets, tightly packed houses. When it got dark, Ben and I used to look at the street lights dotted across the horizon.

"This was where he dumped me," I said.

"I was there, remember?" Tina said.

We walked on quietly. I noticed the tiny bear that was attached to her bag swinging forward. She saw me looking at it.

"Mum bought me that!" she said. "I said, I'm *seventeen*, Mum. I stopped collecting bears a long time ago!"

"How come your boyfriend dumped you?"

"He went to uni one person and came back six weeks later as someone else. Trust me to be involved with the first person on the planet to have a personality transplant!"

I smiled and we made our way towards our street.

"Why don't you come over to my house. Afterwards, I mean," she said, gesturing towards the bag that held the pregnancy test.

I nodded.

"I might need a shoulder to cry on."

"Or someone to celebrate with!"

She went across the street swinging her carrier bag of drugs as though it was lightweight. My bag felt heavy, as if I was carrying some sort of metal – a ball and chain perhaps. When I went in my house there was a Post-it stuck to the hall mirror.

Gone shopping for a few hours. See you. Luv Mum XX

I sighed, pulled the pregnancy test out of my bag and walked upstairs towards the bathroom.

Beverly drove to a house by a park not far from the hospital. Nearby was a busy shopping centre and the streets were filled with yellow lines and permit-only parking. She tutted.

"There's nowhere for us to park, Bobby," she said, threading the steering wheel through her hands as she turned a corner.

The baby was asleep, only its face visible through a tiny peephole of clothes. Beverly glanced down at him and then back to the road.

"You'll love Milly. She's helped lots of babies like you. Maybe they'll find your mummy soon."

She drove around the block without finding a space. When she was nearing the house again a car reversed and then moved out of a space. It was permit-only parking but she decided to take a chance.

The front door of number fifty-two opened before she got to it. Standing there was a small woman wearing jeans with a sweatshirt that had the words *Disneyland Paris* scrawled across the front. Two small girls stood either side of her, identical in every way, right down to their red wellington boots.

"And how are the twins today?" Beverley said, holding the baby carrier in one hand and her briefcase in the other.

"So well behaved," Milly said, putting a hand on each of their heads. "A couple of arguments and a bit of hair pulling but then it's only eleven o'clock."

"Hello," one of the twins said.

"Have you got a baby?" the other said.

"So this is Bobby," Milly said. "Let's get you in, little man."

Beverly followed Milly and the girls along a hallway. From upstairs she could hear the sound of a stuttering trumpet.

"That's Gary. I'm bribing him to do his music practice. It's costing me a fortune but he promises he'll buy me a new house when he makes the big time."

"Is he in a band?" Beverly said.

She walked into a giant kitchen. Along one side of the room were three airers, filled with drying clothes: tops and trousers, pants and socks. Some items were doubled up, others dipped on to the floor. The room was hot and smelled soapy. She placed the baby carrier on top of the table next to three different packets of cereal. Then she took her coat off, fanning herself with a silk scarf.

"Gary's only twelve but I've got high hopes. *Not*." Milly laughed at herself and picked up a pile of clothes from a chair so that Beverly could sit down. The back door opened suddenly and two boys walked in. Their faces were red from exertion and one of them had a ball under his arm.

"Well, Tony, how many goals did you score?" Milly said, brightly.

"Duh!" Tony said. "You don't have goals in baseball."

They walked through, Tony stopping at the fruit bowl, his hand pausing over a banana.

"Have one," Milly said. "And you, Brian."

Brian shook his head furiously and the two boys went out of the room followed by the twins.

"How many children have you got at the moment?" Beverly said.

"Apart from my own two? Let's see," Milly counted on her fingers, "Tony and Brian are here for a few months, maybe longer, and Gary who might be going back to live with his mum in a couple of weeks. That's if she can stay off the booze. Oh and Suzy, but she's at college."

"And now Bobby," Beverly said.

"Oh," Milly said, her shoulders rising with glee, "I do love having a baby round the place. So do all the kids. It really brings out the best in them. Well, apart from the twins."

"Do you ever think that they might not like their mum fostering so many children?"

"No. They love the company and all the *guests* dote on them. They're spoilt silly. How long do you think Bobby will stay?"

Beverly shrugged her shoulders.

"If the mother comes forward, maybe only a few weeks. If not, until they assign Bobby to his adoptive parents."

Milly reached into the baby carrier and lifted Bobby out.

"He's as light as a doll," she said, holding him close to her neck and rubbing his back. "We'll have to put some muscles on you, young man!"

"The doctors think he was a couple of weeks premature. His health is good, though, and he's better here, in a real family, than in the post-natal ward at the hospital."

"Real family, huh! Zoo, more like!"

When Beverly left, Bobby was lying on a quilt on the living-room floor with Milly and one of the twins kneeling by him. She closed the front door quietly, feeling pleased with the situation. Then she looked over and saw a ticket on the windscreen of her car. *Permit-only parking.*

She sighed. She should have known she would get caught.

CHAPTER EIGHT

I didn't need the pregnancy test. My period had already started. I'd had no stomach cramps, no moodiness, no feelings of being bloated. It had just happened, probably sometime when I was walking back from the chemist's with Tina Hicks. I felt my shoulders loosen up, and I lay back on my bed. I wasn't pregnant. I put the palm of my hand over my stomach and felt its flatness. There was nothing there, nothing growing, nothing to be worried about. I was not going to have my life mucked up because of a baby. I sat up and stretched out my arms, feeling my muscles tingling. *Thank you*, I wanted to say. No, I wanted to shout it out, THANK YOU. But there was no one to thank. It was just a freak act of biology. The sperm and the egg had not connected. I'd been lucky.

I got my coat and went across the street to Tina's house. I felt a bit strange standing at her door, pressing the bell, listening hard to see if it sounded. I'd never been there before. She answered immediately and smiled when she saw me.

"Well?" she said.

"It's all right, I didn't even need the test. I've got my period," I said.

"Come in!"

I followed her in. The house was humming with heat from the radiators and I walked on a chunky, old-fashioned carpet down the hallway to the kitchen. I sat at a table in a long thin room with polished wooden floorboards. There were fitted cupboards and a small cooker and fridge. In the corner a washing machine was rumbling quietly.

"Drink?" Tina said

I nodded and just then I heard an upstairs door slam and footsteps descending the stairs.

"Mum," Tina mouthed at me, her forehead wrinkling.

"Tine?"

Marilyn Hicks' voice was scratchy. She appeared a second later and looked very different to how I'd seen her before. Her hair was pulled back off her face and she had no make-up on. She was wearing a light floaty dressing gown belted tightly, making her waist look tiny and her breasts stand out. She kept patting at the belt and she looked upset.

"You want some tea, Mum?" Tina said.

"No, no," she said, shaking her head. "Any phone calls for me?"

"No," Tina said, eyeing me, her voice dropping.

"Oh," Marilyn said, pulling the elastic tie off her hair and shaking her head. Her hair looked wild, as if she'd been in a gale. She noticed me then.

"Hello, Julie," she said.

"It's *Julia*, Mum. She's just come for a chat. . ."

"Ray was going to ring. He said he might. Or he could be busy," Marilyn said, looking at me with an apologetic expression.

Her voice was light and airy, but then it suddenly changed, as though it had dropped into a hole:

"Or he might have no intention of ringing."

"Mum, if Ray said he'd ring then he will."

"Oh, Tine, you're always sticking up for him!"

"Mum, Julia works in a restaurant," she said, "She makes loads of money. It's made me think I want to get a job. Save up for uni."

Tina was trying to distract her. Marilyn seemed to be listening and made a kind of half nod. A second later, though, she stepped over to the wall cupboards and started opening and closing the doors, making tutting sounds, moving dishes around.

"Have a cup of tea, Mum," Tina said, louder, her voice firm.

"What am I looking for, Tine? I've forgotten what I'm looking for."

Tina walked over and put her arm around her mum's shoulder. Without her high heels Marilyn looked tiny. She slumped a bit, her expression relaxing. She looked at me and put her finger up to her temple and made a circular motion.

"I'm going mad, Julie. Don't take any notice of me."

I smiled because I knew she was trying to make a joke.

"It's *Julia*, Mum," Tina said. "Why don't you go in the living room, put the telly on and I'll bring you a nice cup of tea."

Marilyn shuffled off and Tina blew her breath through her teeth.

"She can't get your name right," she said, in an apologetic tone.

"Doesn't bother me," I said.

After taking some tea and toast in to her mum, Tina and I went out. The air was cold and fierce and we headed for the chip shop because I had a sudden appetite. As soon as we turned out of the street Tina seem to relax, shaking her arms and hands as if to keep warm.

"My mum's not mad, you know," she said.

"I *know*. She suffers from depression, my mum said."

"Most of the time she's a completely normal annoying, nagging mother: *do your work; don't take drugs; don't get in too late.* It's just that when things go badly for her she seems to —" she paused, her face screwed up — "to unravel."

I pictured Marilyn in her short skirts and high heels. There was something fragile about her, as if she could topple over at any moment.

"She takes stuff for it?"

"Yep. Loads. The main antidepressants have side effects and she has to take stuff for those as well. If we shook her she would rattle."

There was no queue at the chip shop. I ordered two portions.

"Make mine the low-calorie ones," Tina said, deadpan.

The man looked puzzled. "Do what?"

"Just two portions of chips," I said. "We'll put our own salt and vinegar on."

We walked outside and towards a small swing park at the end of the streets. Just a triangle of ground really, with a couple of swings and a climbing frame. Two boys with bikes were leaning against the metal rungs looking at picture cards, handing them back and forth to each other.

"Tell me about this lad you were involved with," I said, sitting on a splintery bench at the edge of the play area.

"Chris?" Tina said, thoughtfully.

"How did you first meet?"

"Where we lived before? He lived a couple of doors down. He was actually a couple of years older than me and his mum and dad were friends with Mum and Ray. They used to come over a lot, over the years, and me and him were mates."

"What was he like?" I said.

"Tall, chunky like me. Not bad-looking, a bit spotty. He had this great sense of humour, though. He made me laugh a lot."

"Did you go out? What did you do?"

"We spent a lot of time on the computer. Playing games. Going on the internet. Emailing. As soon as I got up in the morning I used to send him an email and he'd reply. One day, you won't believe this, one day we swapped twenty-three emails."

Tina popped a long chip in her mouth and chewed it for a moment.

"I thought I was really close to him," she said, blowing on her next chip. "But when he came back from uni he was a different bloke. He came all the way round my house to dump me. I told him he shouldn't have bothered. He should have sent an email."

"When did you first get together?"

"Last Easter. It was my mum's birthday and Ray had organized a surprise party for her. Chris and me had to make the food during the early evening when mum was out. When Ray rang us about eight we had to lay the food out, put the decorations up, get the neighbours in, all in about twenty minutes flat. Chris was lookout and when my mum's car pulled up we all went quiet. It was a great night. My mum was thrilled, she kept kissing Ray and me and telling us she was the happiest person in the world."

"And?"

"Me and Chris, we went off upstairs. . . You know. . ."

I nodded. I wanted to ask her what they'd done together but I was embarrassed.

"He kissed me. One thing led to another. The computer was on but we weren't exactly playing on it."

"Right," I said, raising my eyebrows.

"I really liked him. Honestly, on that day, when Ray had the party for Mum and I was with Chris it just seemed like everything was perfect. Things don't always stay like that, though."

I shook my head, digging in my paper bag for the last few chips. The two boys had put their cards away and were at the swings, one of them standing on one of the seats, letting the swing rotate so that the chain was twisted up.

"Did you get on with your stepdad?"

"Ray? My stepdad? It's funny but I never really thought about him like that. He was just *Ray*. My mum met him when we were on holiday in Cornwall. He's a surfer."

"A surfer?"

I got an immediate picture in my head of Ray holding a board, legs astride on a sandy beach, the waves exploding behind him. He was wearing baggy trunks with gaudy patterns all over them, just like his shirts.

"He tried to get Mum to do it, but she. . ."

Tina shook her head.

"When he left, just before Christmas, it hit my mum badly."

"I know, my mum told me. . ."

"Nobody really knows how bad it hit her. Not Ray or anybody. I'm the one who sees her at her lowest. Nobody really understands that."

The mood had changed and Tina's face looked heavy. For a second I could no longer see the girl who had got together with Chris while her computer was running in the background. Her chips were only half finished but she screwed the bag up and held it in her palms as though it was a ball.

"I've never said to anyone, but my mum was at rock bottom over Christmas."

I nodded. Out the corner of my eye I could see the boy on the swing twisting round and round, his friend laughing at him.

"We hadn't lived round here long and we hardly went out. I watched her get worse and worse. I tried to get her to go to the doctors but she said, *There's no doctor alive who can mend a broken heart*. She's a bit of a drama queen when she gets going."

"She did go in the end, though," I said, remembering the bag of pills.

"Yeah. Only after she tried to kill herself."

"No!"

"I shouldn't have said that."

Tina stood up and walked across to a litter bin. She chucked her bag in and came back, her shoulders rounded.

"She'd kill me if she knew I'd said that. She denies it, but I'm sure that's what she intended."

"What happened?" I said.

"I woke up on Christmas Eve morning, about seven, I suppose. Just before seven. I went down and made her a cup of tea and took it up to her room. She wasn't there. I shouted out, looked around for her but she wasn't anywhere. I got dressed and ran up and down the street, went round to the corner shop, then here, then to the minicab place. I had no idea where she'd gone."

She stopped for a minute.

"Then I saw her on the footbridge over the motorway. She was standing in the middle at the rail just staring down at the traffic. She was wearing an old summer dress. It was freezing and she just had straps and bare shoulders. From where I was it looked like she was leaning forward and I just ran and ran until I got to her. *Hi Tina*, she said when I was beside her."

"Did you ask her what she was doing there?"

"She said she felt stuffy and just went out for a walk. I took her home. The truth is I didn't want to talk to her about suicide. I couldn't. I just took her home."

"Maybe you're wrong. Maybe she hadn't intended that at all."

"When I got home I found a note from her on my dressing table. I hadn't been looking in my room, that was why I hadn't found it. It was just a scrap of paper and it said. *Dear Tina, I'm sorry, I love you, Mum*."

"Did you ever show it to her."

Tina shook her head and we sat there for a minute.

"Trust me to put a dampener on things!" she said clapping her hands.

"What do you want to do now?" I said.

"How about a walk into the centre. Some shopping? Now that you're not pregnant we can look at the new spring collection!" she said.

I nodded. As we walked away, towards the bus stop, I linked my arm through hers.

CHAPTER NINE

It took me a week or so to pluck up the courage. Tina helped me to get my things together. She said it would be a good way to draw a line under my recent romance. I was nervous but when she called for me at about eight I was waiting. My bag was heavy and I was tense. We walked to school rehearsing it. Neither Ben nor Sara were on the footbridge or at the school gates.

"See if Romeo and Juliet are in the common room," Tina said.

She went off to the library. She was feeling under the weather and was going to sit on the soft chairs near the magazine racks and wait for me there.

It hadn't taken long to find all the things that linked me with Sara and Ben. I'd sat in my room the previous evening and gone through my bag, my drawers and my cupboard. I made two piles on my duvet. Ben's pile was the smaller: a Christmas card that said, *To a Diamond girl, love Ben XXX*; some cinema tickets; a programme for a football match and a Valentine's card. On top sat a maroon satin box – *It's for small pieces of jewellery*, he'd said and I'd foolishly thought he'd been hinting about a ring. Sara's stuff was less personal. A T-shirt that she'd loaned me; a fleece that she'd hung up in my room and forgotten about; a make-up set she'd given me for Christmas and a CD of hers that she'd said I could keep.

I'd packed them into my bag neatly, one thing on top of the other. When I finished I looked round my room with satisfaction. There was nothing of either of them left.

They were in the common room sitting together. Ben had his arm around Sara and he was talking into her hair. She was looking down at her lap and gave a little smile at whatever it was he said. When he saw me walking towards him he seemed puzzled and sat up straight. Sara must have felt the change in him, because she looked up and saw me just as I got to them.

"Julia," she said.

Ben stared straight at me, without a word. A couple of other kids nearby had turned towards them. I could feel their attention on us, a change in the atmosphere of the room.

"I brought your stuff," I said, huskily, my voice on the verge of breaking.

"What. . . You didn't have to. . ."

"I wanted to. I didn't want anything of yours." I looked at Ben, my eyes drilling into him. "Or yours," I added lightly, glancing at Sara, avoiding eye contact with her. "I didn't want any of your stuff dirtying up my room or my house."

I up-ended the bag and the things inside fell out on to the floor. On the top was the satin box; deep purple under the poor lighting of the common room. Sara stiffened when she saw it.

"What's that?" she said, more to him than me.

"Have it. Have all of it. You've got him after all."

Why had I added that? Idiot. Idiot. It hadn't been in the script. I took a breath and gave the stuff a soft kick with my foot and turned to go. As I walked away I heard Sara's whisper, low and angry.

"You gave me one of those bloody boxes!"

I smiled to myself. He'd given her one too. Perhaps he'd said, *It's for small pieces of jewellery*, and she'd seen herself choosing a ring. Only it wasn't that special because he'd bought one for me. I walked out of the building, my bag lighter, my feet moving quickly towards the library to tell Tina what had happened.

CHAPTER TEN

Being friends with Tina meant putting up with Marilyn. She was a kind of drippy presence around Tina's house, always appearing in the kitchen when we were halfway through a drink, pulling Tina's attention away by asking her something that had nothing to do with me. I was nice to her for Tina's sake but mostly she slipped into the background for us.

On Easter Monday there was some unexpected drama. I was at work. It was the busiest day of the holiday. The tables of the Willow Tree were full from twelve-thirty until after four. I hardly had time to think as I rushed from table to the kitchen and back again. My mum was in charge and kept me on my toes, throwing more orders in my direction just to make sure that no one else thought she was giving me an easy time. At four-thirty I sat down in the staff room and took my shoes off. I was exhausted. It was the first chance I had had to rest all day. I picked my mobile out of my bag and saw that I had a message from Tina. *Big Probs Mum trouble*. I pressed her number and in moments she answered.

"Mum's been out all day. I called everyone, her old friends from where we used to live, Ray of course, and even my aunt up in Newcastle. No one had seen her. I didn't know what to do. I was even thinking of calling the police. But then Ray called. He was out with some friends and he saw my mum following him."

"What?" I said.

"It's awful, isn't it? Ray's bringing her home."

"Shall I come over?" I said.

"Yes. No. I don't know what she might be like. I don't know. I'll come over to yours later."

The line went dead and I looked at the phone for a moment as if it had a small screen and I could somehow see what was happening. A picture of Marilyn came into my head, in her high heels, sneaking round street corners, trying to keep up with her ex-husband. It was comical and yet awful. The kind of thing that made you cringe with embarrassment.

I left my mum at the restaurant and got a lift from one of the other workers. I went home quickly and changed. I decided to ignore Tina's advice and go and see her straight away. Her front door opened immediately and Tina stood there looking anxious.

She'd thought it might be her mum, being brought home by an angry Ray. I followed her along the hallway to the kitchen. On the table was a partly eaten sandwich and a glass of orange.

Tina sat down heavily on a chair.

"What happened?" I said.

She shrugged. She put the flat of her hand over her mouth and all at once her eyes glassed over.

"Come on. Don't get upset," I said.

She cried for a few minutes and I stood like a lemon not knowing what to say. I made a move to go round to her but the sound of the front door slamming startled us both. Tina gave a great sniff and sat very still. There were voices and then the sound of feet running up the stairs and other heavier footsteps approaching the kitchen. The door opened and Ray Hicks stood there.

"Tina," he said, looking nonplussed.

Tina stayed in her seat, a tissue bunched up at her mouth. Ray Hicks stood in the doorway and held the palms of his hands out in a gesture of hopelessness. He had a shortsleeved T-shirt over some dark trousers that looked as though they were part of a suit. Oddly, he was also wearing lime green trainers. The kind you could probably see in the dark.

"I'll make some tea," I mumbled, moving towards the work surface and picking the kettle up. I wished

I wasn't there but it was too awkward to make an exit.

"Tina, she has got to stop doing this," I heard Ray say.

"I know, I know. I thought she'd been better lately."

I turned back to watch. Ray was moving his feet about as though he wished he were walking instead of standing in one place. He looked over at me.

"This is my friend, Julia," Tina said.

"You haven't answered any of my emails," Ray said, glancing at me and then back at Tina.

"I've been busy with school and stuff. And I've been looking after Mum."

Tina's voice cracked on the word *Mum*. Ray's face fell. He put his arm out as if he wanted to reach over and soothe Tina. From upstairs the sound of doors opening and closing distracted him and his eyes rolled up towards the ceiling.

"Tina, love. Talk to Mum about going to see the doctor again. OK?"

"Don't worry," Tina said, stiffly, "I know how to look after Mum."

He made a move to walk into the kitchen but then seemed to change his mind. He began to pat at his pockets and then produced a jangling set of car keys.

"You look after yourself," he said.

He had his middle finger pointed at Tina and then he made a double clicking sound with his tongue. He half turned to go and then gave Tina a crooked smile. She just looked at him, her hands clutching the edge of the table. I realized that I was still holding the kettle in mid-air so I turned towards the sink and filled it with water. When I turned back Ray was gone. The front door shut with a bang. She stood up.

"I'd better see if Mum's OK," she whispered.

"Shall I go home?" I said.

I felt superfluous. The atmosphere in the room was gloomy and I suddenly wanted to be back in my own house with my mum, sharing a joke or a bit of gossip.

"No, hang around," she said, going out into the hall. "I'll just check on Mum. Make us a hot drink."

The door closed and I sat down while the kettle boiled, tapping my fingers on the table.

In the last few weeks we'd become pretty good mates. I know Tina didn't *look* like the kind of girl I usually hung about with, and she was a bit too booky for me, always talking about something or other that she'd read (some of which, I have to admit, didn't sound too bad) but she was very mature and always knew the right thing to say. She spent a lot of time on the internet and was always showing me sites that she'd found to do with television programmes that I liked or places I'd been to or colleges that did courses on catering because she thought I wanted to work in restaurants. *If you're going to work in food you might as well be on the creative side,* she'd said. We did searches for our names and I found that there were lots of Julia Diamonds, writers and artists and a jazz singer. I started to look at computers in shops. *We could email each other,* she'd said excitedly and I'd wondered if she was thinking of her old boyfriend Chris.

She'd had an effect on me.

I'm not sure what sort of effect I had on her. She was less isolated and had become more friendly with other kids in school. Not Sara Dewey or Ben Holland. They moved in a kind of no-man's-land for us and we ignored their existence. But other kids who I'd known but who hadn't been part of my previous crowd. They liked her because I did. Then they got to like her for herself. She had a deadpan way of saying things which turned out to be quite funny.

"I see Mr Wilson has been shopping in Bond Street again," she'd say when one of our teachers turned up in exactly the same battered suit that he'd been wearing since the year dot.

"An afternoon with Miss Harris doing Key Skills. What more could a girl ask for?"

It made people smile. And she stopped carrying quite so many books around with her and chatted more.

She also started to diet. This was something I'd felt guilty about. I'd never said anything about her weight, not one word. But since we hung around together she'd started to take more care of the way she looked. I'd noticed some make-up and her hair was more fluffy. Her clothes hadn't changed but I noticed her eating less.

"I need to lose weight. I'm too big at the moment," she'd said.

"You look good though," I said.

"I know I'm big. I can live with that. I'm not fixated with my weight. I don't even weigh myself. But when my clothes start feeling tight then I know I've got to do more exercise, cut down and stuff. I don't want to get any bigger."

I didn't say anything but I did have this kind of fantasy that she would lose the pounds and turn into a thin person. A kind of mirror image of me. Like Sara Dewey? Just thinking about this made me feel bad. How superficial was I? Thin. Fat. What did it matter if you were a nice person? Trouble was, it did matter. You only had to look in magazines and stuff to see that.

She came back into the kitchen wringing her hands.

"She's having a bath. That's the thing with Mum. When things go wrong she retreats to the bathroom," she said.

She shook her head. I heard the kettle bubbling so I got some mugs out and gave her a minute. I was thinking about Ray Hicks and his lime green trainers. He was an odd sort of man. Oldish and yet young at the same time.

"Mum says it was a coincidence. Her being there on the street when Ray was walking along."

"Do you believe her?"

Tina shook her head. Then she started to tell me the story of the day that Ray Hicks left her mum.

"It wasn't a surprise to Mum. They'd decided to split up. That's what Ray said, anyway. I think my mum just accepted that he was determined to go and so went along with the separation thing. He was still living here, sleeping in the spare room. My mum seemed all right about it. I think she always hoped that he would change his mind at the last minute. It took just over a month for him to find a room in a flat and then he told Mum and me he was leaving on the Saturday before Christmas."

I fished the tea bags out of the mugs and dropped them into the bin. I poured milk in and passed Tina's mug across the table.

"Mum tried to persuade him to stay until after the holiday but he was adamant. A couple of days before he was going she suddenly said she was going up to stay with my aunt in Newcastle. It was a relief.

She went off and I was helping Ray to pack his stuff. At least, I thought, being up north, she wouldn't be there when he was moving his things out. At least she'd miss that."

She drank some of her tea.

"It turned out to be the worst day of my life," she said. "Well, except for that other day I told you about."

I nodded. I'd never mentioned what she told me about her mum on the footbridge. I often thought about it though, if I was on my own for some reason, walking high above the traffic, hearing the cars thundering past underneath.

"She turned up just after lunch. Ray had a van parked out the front and everything. We'd even started to move his stuff out. My mum just fell apart. You should have seen her. She was demented. She kept saying, *Don't go! Don't go! Please don't go*. She was begging him, imploring him. I came in from the van and then she started to beg me. *Don't let him go, Tine. Make him stay! Please make him stay!*"

"But he went."

"He went. He couldn't stand it any more. He didn't love her any more. He told me. . ."

She pushed her tea away and it sat in a small triangle with her uneaten sandwich and glass of orange.

"She wouldn't let him walk out of the house. It was awful. She barred the front door, standing there like some sort of guard. *I'm not letting you go!* she said. I tried to pull her away but in the end he just took her by the arm and sort of shoved her to the side. *I'm sorry, Tina*, he said. And then he left. When she realized he'd actually gone she ran out into the street after the van. I'm surprised the whole street didn't hear it."

I hadn't seen that. I'd stopped looking ages before.

"And now she just can't get over him!" Tina said, looking distraught.

I put my hand out to her. I wanted to say *It's her problem not yours* but I knew that was stupid. If my mum were in a state over some man I'd be upset. Tina stood up suddenly and stepped across to the sink. She bent her head over and opened her mouth. She seemed to retch silently. I got up to go over but she shook her head and held her hand out to keep me at bay.

"I'll be all right," she said. "I'm not throwing up. I just don't feel good."

"This stuff with your mum it's making you sick. Maybe *you* should see a doctor."

Tina shook her head.

"Things will sort themselves out," she said, with fake cheerfulness.

I shrugged. What comfort could I give her?

"Look on the bright side," she said, picking up the plate that held the remains of her sandwich. "At least this way I'll be able to lose a bit of weight."

I gave a worried smile as she scraped her food into the bin.

PC Robert Mathews was off duty and wasn't sure what he should wear for a visit to a baby. He put on casual trousers and a jumper but then changed his mind. He tried jeans and a check shirt but after a few minutes took that off and put on his tracksuit. With one last look in the hall mirror he picked up his mobile and his car keys and set off to the address that Beverly had given him.

Beverly was wearing a loose top, jeans and sandals. She'd painted her toenails the same colour as her fingernails. She pulled at the sides of her hair and pushed her fingers through her fringe so that it sat up and looked a little spiky. She looked pretty good for her age. That's what most people said. When the policeman's car pulled up (*Oh, do call me Robbie*, he'd said) she walked out of her front door with a spring in her step. She didn't work on Saturdays but visiting Bobby didn't really count as work.

"There's a couple of developments," Robbie said, as they moved out into the traffic. "You remember the CCTV footage? The builder's van that pulled up beside the car at the lights?"

Beverly nodded, but really she hadn't paid that much attention to the details of the press conference.

"The builder came forward. He said he did remember the car. It was early in the morning and unusual to see many people out at that time, let alone a learner driver."

"A learner?"

"That's what he said. A light-coloured hatchback with L plates and two women in it."

"Will that help?"

"It might well. But there's something else."

"Left here," said Beverly. "About halfway down this street."

"We've received an anonymous tip-off."

Beverly nodded but really she was paying more attention to finding a parking space for him. After getting a ticket outside Milly's she wanted to find a place without yellow lines or permit-only parking.

"It was a receipt for the baby clothes that Bobby was wearing. Every item was on it."

"I remember. A blue babygro and fleece. The poor little mite was dressed for the arctic, never mind London in August."

"Just the receipt inside an envelope. Nothing else."

"Does that help? Oh! There's a space!"

Beverly was gesturing for him to pull over. Robbie eased into the parking space going forward and back three or four times.

"Every little bit helps," he said, pulling the handbrake and turning the ignition off. "Plus the fact that the receipt for the clothes pinpoints the actual time and date of the purchase."

They got out of the car and stood in front of Millie's house. The front door was already open and the twins were standing there.

"It's a chain shop. *The Baby Boutique*. It sells inexpensive stuff."

Beverly walked up the garden path giving the twins a tiny wave. Behind them, coming up the hallway, was Milly with Bobby over her shoulder.

"Oh, look at you!" Beverly exclaimed, putting her arms out to take Bobby.

She introduced Robbie to Milly and the twins.

"He's the man who found Bobby! Rescued him!" Beverly said.

"No," Robbie said dismissively, fiddling with the zip of his tracksuit top and following the chattering group into the house.

Once in the kitchen the twins calmed down and Milly busied herself making some drinks.

"*The Baby Boutique*," Beverly said, picking up their previous conversation, "I know it. How does that help, though? Hundreds of people probably shop there."

"Yes," Robbie said, smiling at the sleepy baby. "Gosh, he looks bigger already."

Beverly nodded, "That's just because you haven't seen him for a couple of days."

"A couple of our officers are going through the shop security videos as we speak. They should be able to get a picture of whoever bought those clothes. Question is, who sent it?"

"Maybe the mother wants to be found," Beverly said, tucking her hair behind her ears and stroking the baby's hair.

"Can I hold him?" Robbie said.

"Course you can," Beverly said. "Mind his head now!"

"I know how to hold babies," Robbie said, indignantly, taking the tiny boy and holding him flat against his Manchester United tracksuit.

CHAPTER ELEVEN

The weeks slipped by until it was warm enough to leave my coat at home and put my boots at the back of my wardrobe. Tina put some of her giant jumpers away and pulled out long-sleeved T-shirts and cotton trousers. Some days we were definitely underdressed but spring was here and we weren't going to turn back and look at winter. Tina and me often stood on the footbridge wearing dark glasses and staring into the horizon. One day the sun was leaning so heavily on my back that I could almost smell the coming summer.

"That's just the fumes from the traffic," Tina said, pulling her glasses down to the end of her nose.

We went for power walks round the local park. It helped her weight, Tina said, and anyway it was good aerobic exercise for both of us. We often saw loads of the kids from school; the boys playing football or just hanging round the snack bar; the girls always somewhere nearby.

Tina's mum seemed to perk up. There were college prospectuses around the house and Tina said she was looking for a course she could do so that she could get a job. Tina was always on employment or college websites printing off page after page of information. Marilyn looked a little bemused by it all but she took the pages, squared the edges and said she was going off to read them. I occasionally found her in my kitchen talking to my mum.

Tina was happy. I asked her once if she'd seen her stepdad and she just said, *Nope, and I don't want to*.

In May we were given study leave to prepare for our exams. Tina had two exams and I had one so we weren't exactly overtaxed. One afternoon, after a gruelling twenty-minute session learning dates and treaties we went to the park and met a couple of lads.

We both had cardboard cups of tea and were leaning against the railings of the small kids' playground. I had a denim jacket on done up to the top button; Tina was wearing a hooded sweatshirt, the hood pulled tightly round her neck for warmth.

"Are we going on this Alton Towers trip or what?" she said.

"When is it?"

"End of June."

I didn't speak. The form group was having an outing to the pleasure park. Everyone was going.

I hadn't made up my mind. Tina seemed to know what I was thinking.

"I suspect Romeo and Juliet will be there," she said. "But you can't let that stop you!"

She was right. I couldn't let the fact that Ben and Sara were going put me off. I was about to agree when, out of nowhere, came these two scruffy-looking lads.

"Get your coats, girls, you've pulled!" the taller one said.

"Pardon?" I said, surprised and dismayed at the same time.

They were wearing jeans and heavy jackets. The taller one had a woolly hat. The other one had cropped hair and a university scarf twisted round and round his neck. They looked as though they were younger than us.

"He's Pete and I'm Greg. You can fight over us later. The loser gets Greg."

I looked away from Pete, my mouth screwed up in fake annoyance. In the corner of my eye I could see him staring at my breasts. Cheek.

"I better tell you though, in all fairness, that Greg here is dynamite in bed. That's what all the girls say!"

I tried to give Pete a cold stare but Tina let out a snorting laugh. I found myself staring at Greg who was nodding sagely and rubbing his knuckle against his cheek as a gesture of achievement. Nonplussed I looked at Tina and joined in with the laughter. I couldn't help it. They'd come out of nowhere, these lads, and had surprised us with their cockiness. We must have been making quite a noise because I saw some kids from our school look around and point at us. Just then Pete pulled his woollen hat off and began to fan himself with it. I looked at his big coat with envy.

"And you are?" Pete said.

"I'm Julia. This is Tina."

"Julia is my favourite name!"

"And I suppose his is Tina?" I said, pointing at Greg.

"No," Pete said. "His is Brigitte. That's bad luck for you! Anywhere round here to go and sit down?"

"Over by the rose garden," I said.

"Fancy keeping us company?" Pete said.

I looked at Tina. *Why not?* I thought.

"Only kissing though," Pete said, "I'm not going any further."

"Oh well then," I said.

I did a wild thing. I couldn't help it. I was drawn to his mirth. I leaned across and gave him a kiss on the lips. It was only a peck and I stood back immediately, amazed at what I'd done.

"So where's this rose garden?" Pete said, looking startled, coughing into the back of his hand.

The four of us walked off, Tina and me in front. She kept pinching me on the arm, whispering, *They're too young!* and I kept elbowing her away.

"Doesn't he speak?" Tina said, finally, pointing at Greg, as we left the snack bar and the kiddie's playground behind.

"Three languages only. French, Spanish and Latin. He hasn't quite mastered English yet."

"What? Are you grammar school boys?" I said.

"'Fraid so. But don't believe everything you read about us. We're not all gagging for sex. Well, Greg is. Hey, look, here we are. The rose garden. How romantic."

We went under an arch of roses into a square patio the size of a tennis court. The middle was full of flower beds. Round the outside were benches. The four of us crammed on to one and we sat awkwardly, me and Tina up one end and the two of them up the other. After a minute of quiet when I began to feel silly, Pete stood up.

"This coat's too hot for me. Hey, Jules, why not come over here and share it with me."

I got up and followed him. Tina had to look after herself. Once we'd sat on the next bench and he'd put his coat round my shoulders I turned and kissed him a couple of times. Why not? He was nerdy but he was making me smile. Anyway, it had been too long since I'd been kissed. I glanced over his shoulder and saw that Tina had the university scarf wrapped round and round her neck and her head on Greg's shoulder. After a while we got up and joined the others back on their bench. Greg didn't say much but Pete told us all about their school with its swimming pool and theatre and state-of-the-art computer rooms and editing suite.

"What you doing round here?" I said, knowing that their school was miles away.

"My dad's come for the cricket," Greg said, pointing into the distance. "We just came along for the ride."

We walked back to the snack bar and had drinks.

"What year are you in, exactly?" Tina said.

"Ten."

We looked at each other and shook our heads. We were hanging round with a couple of fifteen-year-olds.

"We like older women," Greg said.

"What's your mum going to say?" I said, pretending to tut.

"We could get arrested for cradle-snatching," Tina said. "They're just babies!"

But we stayed with them because they made us laugh. We chatted and joked about the comparisons between their grammar school lives and ours. The time flew by and as the afternoon wore on we all fell into an easy companionable silence. We seemed to walk round and round and eventually came to a place where the exit gate was visible. Greg was eyeing his watch. It reminded me that they would be going home soon.

"We have to go," Pete said, zipping his jacket up.

I was about to say goodbye when Pete's arm hooked me round the neck and pulled me towards a hedge and began to kiss me on the mouth. For a second I was going to protest but the kiss sent a spurt of delight through me. I joined in putting my arms around him and pulling him close. When we stopped a few moments later I saw that Greg had his two arms resting on Tina's shoulders and was gently kissing her.

Then, after swapping mobiles and keying in our numbers, they waved goodbye and left.

As we walked out of the park the bubble of pleasure we had had was blown away by a sharp chilly wind. The sun had gone in and it was as if the winter had returned. A car horn was beeping but I took no notice. Then it pulled up alongside. It was my cousin Kath.

"Hey!" she said, calling out of the window.

She was in a car that I hadn't seen before. I remembered my mum saying that she'd recently passed her test and I noticed the green L-plate that was stuck on the bonnet.

"Nice car!" I said.

"Brilliant car!" she said. "Where've you been?"

"In the park."

"All right for some. I thought you had exams?"

"We have. We've been revising."

"With no books?"

"We've been doing some research work," Tina said.

"On what?"

"The differences between grammar schools and comprehensives!"

Kath looked confused.

"I've got some nursing stuff for you, Tina," she said, straightening her rear-view mirror. "I'll bring it over next time I come to tea. Tell your mum I'll give her a ring."

"I will," I said.

We both waved as she drove off. I looked at Tina.

"What you meant was some research on the opposite sex!"

"Someone's got to do it!" she said and we walked off, our arms hugging our chests to keep out the cold.

CHAPTER TWELVE

On the night before the Alton Towers trip we had a celebration. We were both in Tina's bedroom, sitting either side of a bottle of sparkling wine and a large pizza lying in its box. Tina was swigging the wine back and laughing at something I had said. I was cross-legged with a triangle of pizza resting across my hands and was trying to bite a piece so that the topping didn't fall off on to my lap.

The exams were over.

Tina was pulling at a slice of pizza. She'd stopped her diet a couple of days before, saying that it was making her feel funny.

"It's the end of June and I don't feel any thinner. I've cut down for weeks and my clothes still feel tight."

"You look thinner," I'd said, not really sure if she did or not.

"I feel like I've actually put a few pounds on. My breasts feel huge."

"You're lucky. I wish my breasts were bigger!"

"And it makes me feel queasy and gives me all these funny wind feelings in my stomach. . ."

"Wind?" I said, smiling. "Gross!"

"Not *wind* exactly. Just funny feelings in my guts. I don't know. I just don't think it's doing me any good. On top of that I feel tired, like I might be anaemic or something."

"You should join Hypochondriacs Anonymous," I said.

"I can't, I'm too ill to go to meetings."

"Ha, ha. . ."

A slam from downstairs made us both look up. Tina mouthed the words *My mum* as if I thought it might be someone else coming into her house. Her expression changed a second later when a man's voice sounded up the stairs, strong and loud.

"Tina? TINA?"

"Ray's with her," she said, jumping up, walking out on to the landing.

I didn't know whether to follow her or not. I got up and went over to her computer. On her desk she had a pile of printed emails from Greg. Ever since we'd met them in the park Tina had been swapping emails with him every few days. She asked me if I wanted to join in but I told her that fifteen-year-olds honestly weren't my type. I didn't make a big deal of it, though, because she was clearly enjoying herself.

She was downstairs and I wondered what to do. Curiosity made me follow. I'd not seen her stepdad Ray since Easter Monday. I stepped on each stair carefully so that I didn't make a noise. Near the bottom I paused, not sure whether it was right for me to be there. Through the banisters I could see that the kitchen door was shut. Raised voices were coming from behind it. Ray's voice, deep and angry. A high-pitched sound halfway between crying and arguing that I knew was Marilyn. In the middle was Tina, her words steady and calm.

The door opened suddenly and I backed up a few stairs. Marilyn strode along the hallway, her face puce, black make-up under her eyes where she'd been crying. She swept up the stairs as though I was invisible. I felt the silky fabric of her top brush against my arm but I didn't say a word, just kept staring straight ahead with embarrassment. Her footsteps receded and then her room door opened and closed. I heard the key turn sharply as though she thought she might be pursued. Nobody was coming after her, though. For a second I felt this jolt of sympathy for her. I could smell her perfume still lingering on the stairs, sweet and overpowering. Downstairs the kitchen door hadn't closed over and the conversation between Tina and her stepdad continued.

"She has got to keep away from me."

"Mum's not well."

"She's unstable, that's what she is!"

"Don't say that, you don't mean it." Tina's voice was cracking.

"I do mean it, Tina. I do. We're finished. She knows that, yet she's been outside my work three times this week. Just standing in the street looking in at me. People are talking about it! Today I was at a conference in Birmingham. I've only just got back and I find her on my doorstep. *Let's try again, Ray!* If she keeps this up I'm going to the police. . ."

"Don't *say* that. There's no need to *say that*. Mum's been doing great lately. I had no idea that she was even thinking about you. . ."

"She needs to see a doctor. Not just a bloody GP. She needs to see a counsellor or *psychiatrist*."

I stiffened. Ray's voice was hard and dark. In the background I could hear Tina snuffling.

"Give her a chance!"

"That's easy for you to say. You don't have to see her bloody face every time you look out your window."

"Don't talk about her like that."

There was quiet for a moment. The sound of heavy footsteps walking back and forth in the tiny kitchen. Tina blew her nose.

"Oh, Tina, love, come here."

"No! Don't! I don't need you to look after me."

Nothing more was said. From upstairs there was the sound of drawers banging open and shut. I raised myself off the stair, deciding to go back up to Tina's room. I wanted to get out of the way. I heard the sound of the key turning on Marilyn's door, though, so I paused. Then it turned back again as though she couldn't make up her mind what to do. It left me in the middle. I couldn't go up and I didn't want to go down. From the kitchen Ray and Tina began to talk again. This time the tone of their voices had changed. The anger was gone.

"Tina, I'm so sorry to leave you here in this mess."

"It's not a mess. It's my home. It's my mum. I love her."

"I know you do, but she's not right in the head. She hasn't been for years."

"But you loved her for years. You said. . ."

"She's worn me down. You know that. You of all people know what she's like."

"Don't. . ." Tina said.

Their voices seemed to be moving so I stood up and crept back up the stairs. Ray and Tina moved along the hallway.

"I'll get her to go to the doctor's," she said. "I promise. Just don't talk about the police again. Promise me that."

At the front door they stopped and turned towards each other. Tina's stepdad ruffled her hair.

103

"I'll make sure she goes to the doctor's."

Ray nodded stiffly. He looked towards the stairs suddenly and saw me halfway up. I felt immediately guilty and walked down as though I was on my way somewhere.

"You remember Julia? My friend," Tina said, holding her arm out, introducing me as though I was the star of the show.

"Certainly," Ray said.

Under the hall light Ray looked dishevelled. He had an open-necked shirt tucked into dark trousers. I looked down and saw that he had white lace-up plimsolls on. He saw me looking.

"Julia doesn't like my dress style," he said.

"No, I. . ."

"It's all right," Tina said. "You should see Ray's yellow suit. Really."

They were both smiling, as though the unpleasantness hadn't happened, as though there was no trouble between them.

"You liked it when I first brought it home," Ray said, pulling his keys out of his pocket.

"I was only being nice," Tina said.

For a few moments we all stood there. I was taken aback at the sudden good humour. Tina and Ray both had distant expressions on their faces as though they were picturing some scene from their past.

"Your mum thought it was from a charity shop."

"And you said it was from Bond Street."

"It was!"

"You only wore it once!"

"I couldn't stand people staring and pointing in the street."

A voice from behind interrupted the talk.

"That's it. Have a good laugh about me, why don't you!"

We all looked up to the top of the stairs. Marilyn was standing there, her hands hanging by her sides, her mouth in a grimace. Her presence was like a bucket of water over the conversation.

"Marilyn," Ray said, pointing his middle finger at her. "You look after yourself."

"Mum," Tina said, moving towards the stairs.

He turned to the door, clicked his tongue twice and said, "You take care, Tina."

When the door closed I watched as Tina went up the stairs following her mum. I could hear mumbling talk. Tina was trying to make it all all right. It was going to be a hard job. In her room were the remains of our pizza and wine. I didn't feel like either of them. I waited a moment then let myself out and crossed the street. When I got into my house I found a Post-it on the hall mirror that said, **Having an early nite. Wake me before you go to Alton Towers (with a cuppa). Luv Mum XX**

I gently peeled it off and put it in my pocket.

CHAPTER THIRTEEN

The coach to Alton Towers was hot and sweaty. Miss Harris, the teacher who had organized it, was in a strop because there was no air conditioning. The driver, a tall thin man wearing a shirt and tie and dark glasses wasn't bothered.

"It's broken down, Miss. It's either this coach or we would have had to cancel. Your students can open the side windows and once we get on the motorway it will cool down."

Miss Harris marched up and down the coach furiously ticking people off her list and giving the driver fierce looks. Eventually, accompanied by a cheer, the coach moved off and in a short time we were on the motorway. I looked round and was pleased to see that Sara and Ben were up at the back, far away from us.

Tina was feeling unwell.

"It could have been the wine, last night," she said, leaning her head towards the slit of open window.

"Um," I said.

I didn't think it was. Since the previous evening I had formed a good idea why Tina had been feeling odd over the previous weeks. She'd blamed it on her diet: queasy feelings, the fluctuations in her weight, the mood swings. All of those things could be pinned down to stress. She couldn't change the situations between her mum and Ray. The events of the previous evening showed that. So she focused on physical ailments, blowing them up, making them important.

Tina slept most of the way to the theme park and we got there just before eleven. Even though it was a blindingly hot day the air outside the coach seemed cool and I pulled my T-shirt out from my skin and wafted a breeze underneath. Tina was stretching her arms, pulling her hair up and back from her face into a ponytail. Then she let it go and it fell forward making her look hot and bothered. Other kids looked tired and when Miss Harris told us what time we had to get back to the coach people drifted off in small groups. Me and Tina trailed along with some other kids but after a while we paired off on our own.

Tina didn't want to go on any of the fast stuff but we went on the water chute and some of the sillier, slower rides. Around lunchtime, I could see she was tired again. I was feeling hot so we found somewhere shady to sit. Not far away were some lads from our class who were horsing around on the grass. We rolled our eyes at each other as the spray from their water gun cascaded over us.

"Kids!" I said.

Tina didn't respond. She lay back on the grass and put her arm over her eyes.

"So what's Greg saying these days?" I said.

"He says he wants me to go over and spend the weekend at his house."

"Oh!"

Tina had a love life. I didn't.

"You could come. He keeps hinting that Pete would like to see you."

"When he's grown up a bit," I said, sniffily.

"Don't be so choosy. It was fun that afternoon."

"I know," I said, laughing, "It's just that they're . . . immature."

"Wasn't that what made us laugh? What would you rather have? The nice mature Mr Ben Holland who treated you badly? Did he make you laugh?"

I thought about it for a minute. He never made me laugh. I was always in such awe of him; always so grateful for being his girlfriend.

"You're right. Maybe I'll send him a text."

"Well you better get a move on. Greg says he's got his eye on some girl from his horse-riding club."

"*Horse-riding!* That's exactly what I mean. It's not just age. He's a posh brat!"

I had some lunch but Tina couldn't face anything. She drank from a bottle of cold water and sprinkled some of it on her head. Then we went for a walk round, bumping into kids from school. We went on a couple of rides but really our hearts weren't in it. We saw Sara and Ben walking round arm in arm. Tina did a vomit sign with her fingers and we turned off in a different direction. As the afternoon wore on we became bored. Tina was walking slower and I was looking at my watch every few minutes. We'd looked forward to this day but honestly we'd had a better time that afternoon in the park with Pete and Greg. Everyone was due back on the coach by four so we were just hanging around. The park seemed fuller and it was hard to walk without knocking into someone. It made me feel cross, as if I was on the brink of being in a bad mood. Part of the roller coaster was overhead, its carriages shooting past every minute or so, making a shrieking noise that set my nerves on edge. I was about to tell Tina when I noticed that she had turned towards a hedge and was bending forward.

"What's the matter?" I said.

"I don't feel well."

"You're not going to throw up, are you?"

She shook her head and gave a half smile. I turned to go, thinking that was it, that she was all right, and then I felt her lean heavily on me.

"I feel odd. . ." she said.

And she fainted. Right there on the grass she swayed for a moment and then just toppled over.

"Oh, Tina!" I said.

A number of people appeared from nowhere, a couple of girls from school: and then a park security guard walked towards us, talking into a mouthpiece that was hooked on his ear. A woman in a skin-tight T-shirt and cycling pants was kneeling by Tina and turning her on to her side. She had a bottle of water with her and she was trying to sprinkle it on to Tina's face.

Me? I was no help at all. I stood rooted to the spot.

"Is she all right?" I said, to no one in particular.

"She's probably had too much sun," the woman said.

"She'll be fine. Look, she's opening her eyes," someone else said.

"What's happened?"

A loud voice came from behind and I turned to see Miss Harris walking swiftly towards us.

"Tina's fainted, Miss, but she's coming round, I think."

"Oh, poor dear. We'll have to get her to the medical centre. Help her up. Here, Tina, take my hand. Julia, take Tina's other hand. Goodness. . ."

The nurse was in a white overall that had the logo of the theme park on the collar. She looked about twenty-five and her short black hair was gelled so that it sat stiffly on her head, two or three spikes standing up on top.

"What's happened to you?" she said, looking surprised as though the last thing she expected to see were sick or injured people.

"I just passed out. It was nothing," Tina said, looking sheepish.

"I brought her here for you to check over. She may have bumped her head when she fell," Miss Harris said.

"I fell on grass!"

"Better to be safe than sorry, my dear. I'll have your parents complaining if I don't make sure you're all right."

Miss Harris looked at her watch. I looked at mine. It was three-forty.

"Julia, you stay here with Tina. I'm going back to the coach area. When Tina's been checked out you can both meet us there. Hopefully the nurse won't take too long!"

The nurse fingered the spikes on her head, pulling at them gently, so that they had pointed ends. She stared at Miss Harris's back as it disappeared out of the door. Then she turned to Tina.

"Well!" she said, and picked up Tina's hand. "You look a bit worse for wear."

"She's not been all that well, lately. Tell her about the diet, Tina. Maybe that's why you fainted."

The nurse tutted and grabbed hold of Tina's wrist, feeling for her pulse. She looked at her watch and seemed to be counting in her head, her lips only just moving. When she finished she spoke authoritatively. Since Miss Harris had gone she seemed happy to be in charge.

"You girls. Always trying to be thin. Next thing you know it's anorexia!"

"It's not that. I've been really tired. It could be my glands."

"Periods?"

"Not really."

I raised my eyebrows. Tina was seventeen, like me. She'd started her periods. I knew she had. We'd talked about periods.

"I mean I have had periods but they've always been funny, going months between them. Sometimes only spotting."

"Um. I'll just try your blood pressure."

The nurse reached for a small machine with wires and a rubber sleeve attached. She fixed it on Tina's arm. All the while she was talking.

"So quiet today! Just a bee sting and a couple of cuts and bruises. I've had almost nothing to do. Anything serious just gets sent straight off in an ambulance. Most of the time I'm dealing with sunstroke or asthma attacks. And the odd earache."

She pressed the switch on the machine and the

112

rubber sleeve started to swell. Tina was looking better, calmer. She'd probably had too much sun. I looked around the small room. The shelves were almost empty. A small fridge sat in the corner underneath a wall of anti-smoking posters. *Smoking can kill* and *Smoking can harm your unborn baby*. I found myself reading them just to pass the time.

"Um . . . blood pressure's a little high. And I'm just noticing that your ankles have swollen. Do you have problems with water retention?"

"I don't know. I don't think so."

The nurse stood very still with an odd expression on her face. She used her fingers to fiddle with her stiff hair, teasing it out in front of her ears. Then she turned to me.

"Do you mind very much waiting outside? Strictly speaking all medical consultations are private."

"It's OK. I don't mind Julia being here," Tina said, pleasantly.

"I'd rather she was outside, if you don't mind."

"I'll see you in a second," I said, folding my arms across my chest and turning away.

It was cooler outside than before, and I sat on a small wall feeling miffed at having been ejected. I was settling for a longish wait when the door swung open suddenly and Tina stood there, her face in a frown.

"What's the matter?" I said, a sudden feeling of weakness in my stomach.

She started to walk, her face down, her shoulders rigid.

"What's wrong? What did she say?"

"Nothing," Tina said, speeding up, moving away from me, looking up to the right and then left until she located the exit. Then she started to half walk, half run towards it. In the distance I could see Miss Harris waiting, her face breaking into a smile when she saw us.

"Tina, what did she say? She must have said something!"

We reached Miss Harris before I could get another word out of her.

"We're late, girls, let's go. Are you all right, Tina? Good, let's get going."

Everyone was already seated on the bus and there were a few jeers as we got on and made our way down the aisle towards our seat. Some of the boys made rude comments about what we'd been doing so I told them where to go.

"Language, Julia, please," Miss Harris's voice rang in my ears.

"What's wrong?" I hissed.

We had only just sat down as the coach started moving out of the car park. Miss Harris was counting out loud as she backed up the aisle towards the front.

Tina shook her head from side to side.

"Are you ill? Does she think you're ill?" I

whispered. "Did she tell you to go and see your doctor?"

Tina nodded, her lips tightly pursed together, her arms and shoulders feeling tight and hard against mine. I wanted to put my hand on hers to break her mood but she seemed untouchable. Then I saw her eyes glass over and she blinked out a tear.

"Honestly!" I said, feeling my temper rising. "What on earth did she say?"

"She said," Tina said, in a snuffled whisper, "she said I should go and see my doctor because I might be pregnant."

"What?"

She just looked at me in a sullen way. She didn't need to repeat it. *Pregnant*. I heard it right the first time.

AUGUST 26th

The CCTV footage from the shop, *The Baby Boutique*, was poor quality but at least it hadn't been taped over. Detective Inspector Frank Sullivan had had copies made and the pictures sat on a pile in front of him. Across the top was a headline. **Do You Know This Woman?** He wanted it to be eye-catching. It had been six days since the baby had been found and there hadn't been a word from the mother. The story was going cold and the public were losing interest.

He was sitting at his desk, preparing to eat his lunch. In front of him was a plastic box with a dark blue lid. He levered it off to see what Jeanie, his wife, had prepared for him. A wholemeal sandwich and an apple. A small tin foil package was wedged in the box and Frank's eyebrows shot up. Olives. He hadn't known that Jeanie had bought them.

Across from his desk was a television on a trolley. He picked up the remote and pressed a button. The screen wavered and then a fuzzy picture appeared. The inside of a shop. Carefully unwrapping the clingfilm around his sandwich he pressed the fast forward button and took a bite while he kept his eye on the time indicated in the bottom left hand of the screen. He stopped the tape at 12:02pm. He allowed the video to run at normal speed and took another bite of his sandwich. Tuna mayonnaise with just a touch of spring onions. Perfect. Jeanie knew exactly what he liked.

His office door opened and Robert Mathews came in. Frank liked Robert Mathews. He was an enthusiastic copper and didn't worry about clocking in and out. Robert didn't stop work just because he was off duty. He'd been in virtually every day since he found the baby to see if the mother had contacted them.

"This the footage?" Robbie said.

He was standing looking at the television. Frank's mouth was full so he nodded. Undoing his foil pack of olives he pointed to the time at the bottom of the screen.

"12:06pm. That's what we're interested in. The receipt for the baby's clothes was actually 12:10 but the woman comes in and browses for a few minutes before she pays for the items. You don't get that good a look at her until she's just about to leave. Look, here she comes, striding into the shop."

"You think she's the mother?" Robbie said.

"No. Don't forget this was most likely shot a day after the baby was born. This woman looks fit and energetic. I'm guessing that women aren't this active on the day after giving birth. I couldn't say for sure because Jeanie and I, we haven't had any children."

117

"Do you think she sent the receipt in?"

"Hard to say."

"She's having a good look around," Robbie said.

"Now she's picking up a basket. You lose her a bit here because these school kids are in the way. Someone told me you'd seen the baby? How is the little chap?"

"Bobby's fine. I'm sure he smiled at me."

"That's a fallacy. Babies don't smile before they're six weeks old. Jeanie read that on an internet site. It was probably wind!"

"There she is," Robbie said, pointing. "At the front of the shop. In the light from the street."

"She's queuing up now," Frank said, picking a single olive from his lunchbox, biting into it gingerly in case there was a stone.

"So, right at this moment, the mother, whoever she is," Robbie said, narrowing his eyes to focus on the woman waiting to pay at the till, "is at home, after having given birth to a baby?"

"We can only speculate. Young girl most likely."

"Probably in need of medical help?"

"Ah, maybe that bit of the mystery will be solved for you in a moment," Frank said, folding up the piece of foil into a neat square and replacing it in the plastic box.

The video showed the till point and some of the shop beyond. The woman, whose face was still a little fuzzy, was at the front of the queue and had placed her basket on the counter. The shop assistant was scanning the goods and the woman pulled some money from a pocket.

"Here you are," said Frank. "This is where her jacket or coat opens."

The woman appeared to be hot and she pulled at the corners of her jacket fanning herself. Then she pulled them back as far as they would go without coming off her shoulder. The shop assistant counted out her change.

"See?" Frank said.

He'd seen the tape a dozen times so he knew what he was looking for. Robbie looked puzzled.

"She's wearing a uniform. A *nurse's* uniform."

"Oh!"

"If she's a nurse and she's linked to the mother, maybe she's made sure that the girl, or woman, has had medical attention."

"I see, I see," Robbie said.

Frank was pleased. It was a good clue. It was a fuzzy image but the shop in question was fairly close to the local hospital. They could put posters up there today and who knows, maybe they'd have a name pretty soon.

After the young policeman had gone Frank sat back and ate his apple. It was crunchy, the sort he liked. When he'd finished he rang Jeanie to tell her how he'd enjoyed his lunch. As ever, she wanted an update on the abandoned baby story. *How could anyone give their baby away?* she said, sadly. After he put the receiver back he thought about that for a moment. He and Jeanie would give anything to have a baby. And here was a woman, or a girl, who had simply dumped hers on the street. He couldn't help but feel the tiniest bit angry.

CHAPTER

We stepped off the coach at just after seven and Tina walked off without saying goodbye to anyone. Some girls asked what was wrong and I just shrugged my shoulders. They were all going to a local pub but I shook my head and went after Tina.

On the coach I'd tried to get her to talk about it. I'd reassured her that she *couldn't* be pregnant. She'd nodded her head from time to time. She'd hardly said a word, though, and I couldn't even be sure that she'd heard half of what I'd said. For most of the journey she'd made a pillow out of her sweatshirt and leaned it against the glass and kept her eyes closed.

"How could you be pregnant?" I'd whispered. "You haven't seen Chris since before Christmas!"

I tried to convince her but then I realized that I was also trying to convince myself. She'd missed her periods. She'd been feeling sick. Her breasts had got bigger and even though she'd been dieting she hadn't lost any weight. Plus she was tired all the time.

"I'm all right," she said, when we finally got back to our street. "I just need a bit of time on my own. I'll see you tomorrow."

I was left standing at the end of her garden path as her front door shut. I had no choice but to go home. My mum wasn't in so I started to make myself a cup of tea, but just as the water boiled I changed my mind and went into the living room, slumped down on the settee and put the television on. I was hot so I got up and opened the living-room window. The net curtain rippled in the stiff evening breeze and I stood there for a moment and felt the cool air on my face. Tina's house looked quiet and I wondered what she was doing at that moment. There was a feeling of frustration building up inside me. I sat back down and clicked the remote from one channel to the next. I lay back. I turned over on my front. Then I stood up and turned the television off and slung the remote behind me.

I had to *do* something. How could she expect me to just leave it? The nurse's words, which had seemed ludicrous, now looked more and more likely, and yet at the bottom of everything was this big hole. How could she be pregnant? We'd been friends for months, and apart from an afternoon with a couple of schoolboys at the park there'd been no male company. If anyone was pregnant it should be me! Wasn't that how we got together? How we became friends? In the chemist shop with Tina picking up my pregnancy test?

I clapped my hands. The pregnancy test!

I raced up to my room and found it at the back of my wardrobe. I took it downstairs, dropped it into a Tesco carrier bag and went out. I virtually marched across the road, determined to see her. When Marilyn answered the door, I said, *Hi Marilyn, Just got to see Tina for a minute* and walked straight past. She mumbled something about Tina having a headache or too much sun and I ignored it. I went upstairs, knocked lightly on her door and went straight in. I didn't want to give her the chance to say she didn't want me there.

Her room was in semi-darkness and she was lying on her bed. I didn't turn the light on but I went over and sat down. I could feel the heat coming off her and I could see that she'd been crying.

"Tina, I've brought this."

I tipped the box out of the carrier bag: *Expectations – Pregnancy Testing Kit.* She picked it up, turning it over. She leaned up on her elbow.

"It's simple to use. And then you'll know for sure," I said.

"Is there any point?" she said.

She sat up. Her arms felt damp and her face was red from crying.

"I'll wait in here," I said. "It only takes minutes. That's what it says on the packet."

She plodded out of the room and I heard the bathroom door shut. I had a heavy feeling in my chest. *Tina Hicks pregnant!* From her expression, from the way she took the box, I knew it would be positive. She knew it too. What I didn't know was how or when it had happened. Had Chris come back to see her in the spring? Had there been someone else? There were questions twitching in my head. Why didn't I know about it? Why was I in the dark? Weren't we supposed to be friends?

It seemed like she was gone for a long time. I turned her bedside light on and noticed her computer screen had fishes swimming across it. I walked over and looked at her desk. Her school folders stood up against the wall in an orderly line, each one with a small label on its side indicating what it was for. I thought of my own stuff, in a pile at the bottom of my wardrobe. I moved her mouse and the fishes disappeared and instead there was an email on screen that she had already opened. It was from her stepdad Ray, just a few lines and my eyes flicked over them.

Good to see you Tina even in such depressing circumstances. Look after your mum. I know how much she depends on you. Love Ray.

124

He had an odd signature line at the bottom.
Surfers Do It On Board!!!
Ray Hicks Big Wave Computer Support Services
Just then the door opened and she came back into the room. She was holding the test in one hand.

"It's positive. I knew it would be. When that nurse said it today I thought, *Duh, idiot, idiot.* I . . . we . . . never used any protection. Of course there was a chance, a possibility. . ." she said, sniffing, wiping her eyes with the back of her other hand.

"I don't get it," I said. "I thought you and Chris finished before Christmas. Did you see him again? You didn't tell me!"

"The last time I saw him *was* just before Christmas."

"But. . ."

"I thought, afterwards, in January that something might have happened," she said in a loud whisper. "But then I had this short period, a day, half a day, something like that. I assumed it was OK. I just thought it couldn't have happened to *me.* I crossed it out of my mind. I didn't have a period for a while then but there was some spotting round about Easter. I'm sure there was. That's what I'm like. I've never had regular periods."

I wasn't really listening. She'd seen Chris before Christmas. That was over six months ago.

"All the other things, feeling sick, my breasts getting bigger. I did consider it. That weekend when you and me got friendly. When you were carrying the test home from the chemist's. I thought about it then. But only in a sort of distant way. Wouldn't it be funny, I thought, if I was pregnant? But it was so funny that I just dismissed it. After all, if I was pregnant, wouldn't I have a great lump sticking out of my stomach?"

"Six months. . ." was all I could say.

I looked at her, sitting on the edge of her bed, her shoulders rounded, her breasts heavy, the fabric of her T-shirt camouflaging her stomach. There was a baby inside her. How could she not have known?

"All the other things," she continued, as if sensing my disbelief. "My weight. Well, so what? I've always been big. My weight goes up and down. That wasn't unusual. I was feeling lousy, tired and depressed, but you know, with Mum being all over the place I put it down to that."

All that time when I was worried about myself I'd watched her walking around, a model of ordinariness. A *nice* girl. Not exciting, not my sort. And she'd been carrying a baby inside her like a folded-up secret.

"You're over six months pregnant," I said.

I sat on the bed beside her. I watched as she slid the test back into its box and then into the Tesco carrier bag, wrapping the plastic round and round. When I bought it, all those months before, I had two options. To keep the baby or have an abortion.

Tina had no options. Her baby was there in the room with us; a third person, silent and waiting.

CHAPTER FIFTEEN

The two weeks following our Alton Towers trip were unreal. It was as if we'd stepped out of the everyday regular world. At first Tina stayed at home, mostly in her room, wrestling with the new situation that she had found herself in. After that, with some persuasion, she ventured out. Everything else went on as normal. My mum went out to work. I waited on tables in the Willow Tree. I went to the supermarket. Kath came round for tea. My mum brought fish and chips home. Tina's mum went out shopping; buying things for a holiday that she'd organized for herself and Tina. When I went over Marilyn opened the front door, giving me a nice smile and telling me that Tina was upstairs. Everything was *normal*.

Once inside Tina's bedroom her situation dwarfed everything else. She looked immediately bigger to me. As though overnight her bump had appeared. She had a tiny baby inside her, curled up, oblivious to the trouble it was going to cause. Her breasts looked heavier and she seemed to be constantly crossing her arms to hide them. She was physically substantial; like a woman, not a teenager. I suddenly felt strange with her, like I couldn't make any silly jokes or talk about the kind of subjects that usually obsessed us: boys, music, careers, plans for the future. What was the point? A tiny bomb had been thrown into Tina's life. Why should she care what sort of jeans I wanted to buy?

My first suggestion was that she should tell her mum but she shook her head vehemently at this. Then I said that she should go to the doctor's but that only made her cry. I suggested talking to Kath, who was a nurse and would know what to do, but she just stared down at the floor and didn't answer.

"You can't just do nothing!" I said, frustrated.

She shook her head and wiped away her tears.

In the end I said nothing and decided to bide my time. *Give it a couple of days for her to get used to it*, I thought. It wasn't like there was any kind of hurry. She still had months to go and at some point she would have to tell someone because it would become obvious that she was pregnant. As soon as I stopped nagging her to tell someone she became more relaxed. She turned that first week into a kind of fact-finding exercise. She clung to her computer, visiting various websites, and we both began to know more about the course of a pregnancy. It was forty weeks, not nine months as I'd always thought. By twelve weeks all the basic bits were formed: arms, legs, fingers and toes; facial features and shape. She said she was six months, which meant it was much bigger and moving around, which explained the peculiar feelings she'd had in her stomach in the previous weeks.

The womb or *uterus* started off the size of a pear and ended up as a great balloon full of fluid in which the baby floated. When she came to full term the baby would have to be pushed out. Neither of us said much about that.

I asked her about Chris.

"Don't you think he'd want to know?" I said.

"I'm not telling him," she said, chewing on her nail.

"Why?"

"I don't want him involved."

"But doesn't he have a right to know? As it's his baby?"

She didn't answer. That was how it was. If she didn't want to talk she just turned back to her computer.

"You can't do it by yourself," I said, softly.

"I just can't make any decisions now," she said, her voice full of irritation.

She was often difficult to fathom. She saw me

every day that I wasn't working and we spent a fair bit of time together, but it was hard to know what was going on in her mind. I spent a week giving in to her, avoiding any conflict, pampering her with treats and magazines, as if she was a sick person. She was going on holiday the following weekend. Surely, I thought, she would tell her mum before then. Some days I felt quite upset about it all, others I found myself in a state of awe about the information that I carried round. I held it deep inside, a jewel of a secret. I was the only one who knew. What would other kids in school think? What would my mum say? Tina was my friend and I felt sorry for her but I also had this information in me that would shock and surprise just about everybody. It made me feel a little bit light-headed. After a week, when she hadn't told anyone, the knowledge began to weigh a little heavier. Everyone was going about their business unaware of Tina's bombshell. Nothing had changed; life was continuing. Tina was going on as though nothing unusual was happening with her. I began to feel a mild sense of panic. *She had to tell someone!*

We went out one day in the second week so that she could buy some stuff for her holiday.

"Can you imagine it? Me, my mum and my auntie Sheila in a mobile home at Bridlington."

"Where's that?" I said.

"Perched on the edge of the North Sea. We've been before. It's usually pretty windy and you need to wrap up warm. That's in July, of course. The rest of the year you need thermals."

I was astonished how she could talk so – as if she was just a regular teenager going on holiday. Not six months pregnant. How could she just ignore it? We sat in a coffee bar after she'd bought some tops and I couldn't keep my thoughts to myself.

"You have to tell your mum. Now, today. You can't go on acting as though everything's normal!"

I thought she would stare off into the distance or shrug her shoulders or blink a few tears out. She didn't though.

"I will tell her. Before we go on holiday, I'll tell her."

"Good," I said. "It's for the best."

But she didn't tell her. Not that day or any other day that week. I found myself pacing up and down my room wondering whether to go and tell my own mum. The knowledge of Tina's pregnancy became something huge and unwieldy that I was dragging round with me; a heavy stone that was making my shoulders stoop and my head hang.

On the day before she was due to go on holiday I insisted that she did something. We were in her room as usual and Marilyn was vacuuming downstairs. I could hear the machine roaring and hitting the skirting boards. Tina was wearing a dress that I hadn't seen before. Over the top of it she had a loose blouse, only one button done up. It gave the illusion of shape.

"Why won't you tell your mum? I don't understand!"

"You know how fragile my mum is. If I tell her about this it will just add to her worries."

"But it might be the very thing that pulls your mum out of herself. If she's got you to worry about then it'll take her mind off Ray."

"Depression doesn't work like that. She can't just file her feelings for Ray until she's sorted my problems out. Everything gets thrown together and weighs her down more."

The vacuuming was moving up the stairs. Every now and then it was switched off and we could hear Marilyn carrying the machine up a couple of steps.

"But you need her now," I said, lowering my voice. "Remember that time when I thought I was pregnant? My mum was the first person I would have told."

"But in the end you told me, remember?" Tina said. "That's why I'm telling you. I will tell my mum. Honestly. When I'm on holiday. When my auntie Sheila's there. I'll tell her then. I promise."

The vacuuming was outside the door. Suddenly the sound stopped and the place was silent. Tina cocked her head, listening. A moment later we heard Marilyn humming.

"When she's all right, I'm all right," Tina said, turning back to the computer and moving on to a young mums' website.

That afternoon I went out by myself and wandered round the shopping centre. After a while I found myself in WHSmith in front of a row of magazines that had to do with pregnancy. I flicked through some of them and read what snatches of articles that I could. *Caesarean or Natural Birth. Pain Relief, To Have or Have Not. The Eighteen-Hour Labour. Breast is Best. Multiple Births.* Afterwards I walked home. Everywhere I looked there seemed to be pregnant women around. The heat meant that they were wearing T-shirts and drawstring trousers or light, almost see-through, cotton dresses. They all seemed huge, their bump rising out from beneath their breasts and looking big enough to unbalance them. Where I could see their midriffs, the bump was as smooth and round as marble, the belly button rising in the middle like a bubble.

The next morning I popped over to say goodbye to Tina and her mum.

"I've told you," she said, standing beside a line of bags in the hallway, "I will tell her. When she's relaxed."

I could hear a radio from upstairs and the sound

of Marilyn's heels stomping around. Tina was wearing some loose trousers and a long blouse which was hanging open over a T-shirt. She'd just phoned for a cab and was a bit agitated, patting a small bag that was hanging diagonally across her front. She suddenly stopped what she was doing and put her hand on her stomach.

"Are you all right?" I said, concerned.

"Give me your hand," she said, glancing upstairs and turning away, into the wall. "Here."

She took my hand and placed it firmly on her stomach. It made me feel silly and I tried to pull away but she held tight.

"Just wait for a few moments. . ."

The radio had gone off and the hallway was quiet. I could hear Marilyn on the landing upstairs mumbling to herself. And then I felt it. A tiny movement. A silent thump. Once, twice, three times. Then again, twice in succession. When it stopped Tina let go of my hand. The skin on her stomach was warm and my hand felt cold when I took it away.

"That was the baby?" I whispered, a touch of awe in my voice.

She nodded. Her mum was coming down the stairs.

"Don't worry about me," Tina said, in a low voice.

"Hi Julie!" Marilyn said.

Tina rolled her eyes. Her mum would never get my name right. I helped to carry their cases outside and then I left them as their taxi turned into the street to pick them up.

CHAPTER SIXTEEN

Tina and her mum were a few hundred kilometres away. I'd had a few calls from her but mainly to say that she'd arrived and to tell me about the caravan park and the stiff breeze from the North Sea. She didn't mention the baby and neither did I. It seemed too huge a subject to fit into a mobile phone conversation. I asked her if she was feeling OK and she said she was. That was it. A tiny exchange that covered up a massive awkward silence. She sounded quite happy. I asked her how her mum was and she said she was great, that she was really enjoying her sister's company and looking better day by day.

I still felt burdened by their situation. In Tina's absence I found myself round-shouldered and irritable. I bit my mum's head off several times and felt lethargic and tired. At work I got some orders mixed up, bringing the wrong dish to a number of people and getting the drinks muddled. I was also scowling a lot and several people asked me if I was all right.

I wondered if Tina was feeling like that. And then I pictured her on some beach path, her mum in high heels and a short skirt, walking along with Sheila (who I imagined to look a bit like Marilyn). There'd be seagulls swooping here and there and making a terrible squawking sound, and families coming the other way holding balloons or candyfloss. Marilyn and Sheila would be talking, linking arms, and Tina might be a few metres behind, her hands holding the edges of a loose shirt that wanted to fly back. What was Tina thinking? That's what I wanted to know.

At the beginning of the second week I got another call from Tina.

"I can't talk long. I haven't got much credit. I'm fine and Mum is great. You wouldn't recognize her. She's talking about seeing this counsellor when we get back, and guess what? She's made up her mind about a computer course at college so that she can get a job. I've really got a good feeling about it."

"And you're going to tell her," I said, and lowered my voice, "about the baby?"

"Yes, I will, when I get back home."

"You said you'd tell her when you were away. . ."

But the line went dead. She was out of phone credit.

It put me in a terrible mood. I hardly bothered with myself, grouching around the house, sniping at my mum.

"What's wrong with you!" she demanded, when I raised my voice for something stupid.

"Sorry, Mum!" I said, "I've got some things on my mind."

"Exam results?" she said, looking concerned.

I nodded. It was easier than making my own story up.

On my way to work on the Thursday before Tina was due to come home I saw Sara Dewey. I was in a clothes shop mindlessly looking along the rack of tops when she patted me on the shoulder.

"Oh hi," I said, surprised.

"I thought it was you. Seen anything nice?"

She looked thin, the bones of her shoulders showing outside the straps of her T-shirt. Her hair was different. She'd had it cut and it was jaw-length, like mine. She had a straw bag over her shoulder that looked heavy.

"No, just looking. I'm just on my way to work."

I walked towards the doors of the shop and she came with me.

"Still at the Willow Tree?" she said.

I nodded. I took a few steps wanting to get away from her. Not because I had any bad feelings left towards her but because she seemed part of a previous life. We had nothing in common and I had other things to think about. I was about to say *See you* when she put her hand on my arm and stopped me.

"Me and Ben broke up a couple of weeks ago," she said. "I thought you might like to know."

It stopped me. In that second, standing outside the clothes shop, a load of questions popped up in my head. *How? Why? When? What did he say? What did she say? What was the reason?*

"It was a mutual decision. You know. It wasn't really working out."

And then I understood. Her eyes were boring into me, wanting me to read something into her words. Her body language was full-on, her hand on my arm, leaning towards me, searching out my face for a response. She wanted me to be her friend again.

"Sorry to hear that," I said, stepping back, out of her reach. "I have to run, I'm late."

I left her there and didn't look back.

I finished my shift at work about seven and got the bus home. Walking into my street I fished my front-door keys out of my bag and had them ready. Before I got to my door, though, I heard the hooting of a car horn.

"Over here!"

It was my cousin, Kath.

"Jump in," she said. "Come for a ride."

I began to shake my head but she'd leaned across and opened the passenger door.

"Come on! Chop chop!" she said.

After a moment's hesitation I got in and she made a great show of checking that my door was shut and telling me where my seat belt was. After indicating and looking over her shoulder four or five times she finally moved out into the street and drove slowly down the road.

"We'll go to the forest."

We parked on an area of stony ground next to a twenty-four-hour snack bar. It was almost eight o'clock and I'd not eaten. I bought a drink and a roll. Kath had a drink. As soon as we sat down, me on one side of a picnic table, she on the other, it came into my head that I should tell her about Tina. She was talking about a male nurse in her ward who thought he should be in charge because he was older than her. They'd started together though, she went on, and she'd done as much study as he had, but. . .

I let her talk on and imagined what it would be like if she knew. Immediately I felt this lightness in my shoulders. She wasn't a mum or anyone who was in charge of me or Tina. She certainly didn't know Marilyn or Ray. On the other hand she was older than me and more responsible, and a nurse as well. By telling her I was drawing Tina towards the medical world.

"What you smiling for?" Kath said, looking puzzled.

I felt it build up inside, like I was on the edge of a diving board at the swimming pool and I was swaying back and forward, wanting to jump in but being afraid at the same time.

"My friend Tina is pregnant. Not just pregnant but six months pregnant, and she won't tell anyone." I blurted it out.

Kath stared at me, her big cheerful face dropping. "Shit," she said.

I told her the rest. It was jumbled up and I repeated myself a number of times. The main thrust was clear though and Kath's face, usually so positive and pleasant, looked dark and baffled.

"How could she not have known?" she said, leaning her chin on the palm of her hand.

"I didn't even know that she'd . . . you know . . . done it!"

"The quiet ones. . ." Kath said, tapping her fingers on the wooden table.

"She won't even go to the doctor's. I mean she's seventeen. They'd have to keep it confidential but she won't even go there!"

I shook my head as a motorbike roared up and parked in the car park next to Kath's car. The motorcyclist stood beside it in his leathers and took a moment to take off his helmet. Then he shook his head, his hair wet with sweat. I'd expected someone young but he was grey and hunched. His bike was leaning to one side looking worn out.

"What should I do?" I said, the words just flowing out. "I'm trying to, you know, support her, but I'm getting worried. There must be tests she should have, examinations. She needs to see a midwife, doesn't she? You're a nurse. You know what she needs to do."

"Why is she so against telling her mum?"

I told Kath about Marilyn's feelings for Ray and how it was sending her over the edge. I explained about her bothering her ex-husband and how he'd threatened to go to the police. Out of the corner of my eye I could see the aging rocker. He was peeling an orange and eating the segments one by one.

"Tina's worried whether her mum will be able to cope."

"It depends how bad Tina's mum's depression is. On a good day it might be an important bit of news for her. It might very well shake her out of her preoccupations about her ex-husband."

"On a bad day?"

"Hard to say. Maybe Tina is waiting for the best time. She knows her mum better than anyone, after all."

"You think I shouldn't push her?"

"I honestly don't know. She'll be, what? Thirty-two or -three weeks when she comes home? That's a long way along. She *should* see her doctor."

"She says she'll tell her mum on Saturday, when they get home."

"Why not wait and see what happens. I'll tell you what though, she should tell the father, this university lad. Why should he get away with it scot-free? It takes two to make a baby!"

Afterwards Kath dropped me off and I made her promise again that she wouldn't tell a soul about Tina. She turned the ignition off and pulled her mobile out of her bag and handed it to me.

"Here, key your number in. Give me yours and I'll do the same. When Tina gets back she might want a chat. Especially if her mum blows her top. Then you can get me anytime."

I gave her my mobile and put my number in hers. I waved her goodbye as her car stuttered down the street. It was almost nine-thirty but Mum was still at work. I went in and sat down in the darkened living room. Kath had said a load of reassuring things and I felt glad that I'd told her. Tina's secret was lighter now that Kath knew as well.

They arrived back late Saturday afternoon. I saw the taxi pull up as Mum and me were on our way out for an evening shift at the Willow Tree. I dashed across to say hello. Marilyn looked tanned. When I said it she roared with laughter and said it was more likely to be rust with the kind of weather they'd had. Tina looked fresh-faced and happy. She also appeared a lot bigger.

Whether she was or just *looked* bigger because I hadn't seen her for two weeks I didn't know. I told her I was going to work and she said she wouldn't come over later but she'd see me the next morning. I was relieved in a way. I wanted to give Tina time to tell her mum about the baby. Maybe, by the next morning, everything would be out in the open. That's what I thought.

"Is Tina putting on a bit of weight?" my mum said as we drove off.

Frank Sullivan had three names on his list. These had been whittled down from a longer list of possible sightings of the blurred nurse in the CCTV footage.

He was sitting in a small interview room in the King William General Hospital. Beside him, on another soft chair, was Beverly Ward, the social worker assigned to the baby. Frank cleared his throat and straightened his tie. He always felt a bit awkward with Beverly. She was taller than he was, for a start, and regularly had her nails painted in some flamboyant manner. They usually stood out against whatever documents or files she was looking at: blood red some days, pearl blue or sea green on others. It was disconcerting to see a professional worker place importance in such matters. His wife, Jeanie, would never waste her time on such things.

Two of the names on his list had been crossed off. Both nurses had been friendly and helpful but had no links to the baby. Beverly had shown them the book of photographs anyway. Ten pictures in a small blue album which Beverly and the foster parents had taken between them. The nurses had smiled delightedly, looking at the tiny baby.

They were waiting for the last name on the list. Katherine Pickford, they'd been told, was on duty in Iris ward and had been informed that they were waiting to talk to her. Even if she turned out not to be the one there was still hope that someone else in the hospital might recognize the image from the CCTV. Sometimes it took a few days for an image to register.

"How is the little lad?" Frank said, glancing at his watch.

It was almost six o'clock. Frank had intended to visit the hospital earlier in the day but had been obliged to attend a conference on *Community Policing in the Twenty-first Century.*

"He wasn't too well yesterday. A bit of colic, I think. He ran a temperature but the foster carer took him to her doctor's and I think everything is OK."

Beverly had the album on her lap and her hands clasped on top of it. Her nails, Frank noted, were a pale shade of orange.

"May I?" he said, holding his hand out for the photos.

He opened the album and looked through. He grinned to himself. The baby had saucer eyes with long lashes and pale skin, with just a hint of dark hair on his head. Hadn't Frank read somewhere that a human being's eyes were the same size at birth as they were for an adult? Wasn't that why they seemed so big in babies? Beverly had taken most of the shots herself and the baby was usually propped up on someone else's lap although a couple were taken of him laying on a rug on the floor, his arms stretched out as though he was running into the finishing tape in a race.

Beverly reached down into her bag for her diary. She opened it at the current week and glanced through her appointments. The following day she was due to go to a case conference where the baby's future would be discussed. Adoption. That was the next step, assuming the natural mother didn't come forward. It would all take time, though. Somewhere there was a couple who were waiting for a baby of their own. They most probably had a room for a nursery set aside. Beverly knew the types. She had been on a couple of panels where prospective parents had been assessed. They were generally nice, warm people, but there was often a hint of desperation about them. They'd tried for years to have their own baby and then they'd had to give up. This process, this waiting for a baby to adopt, was their last chance.

The police inspector's voice broke into her thoughts.

"This is a good one," he said.

He was looking at the picture where Bobby was sitting on Robbie Mathews's lap. Not that anyone else would know it was Robbie because his head was cut out of the shot. The baby had his Manchester United all-in-one suit on and somebody, one of Milly's children perhaps, had placed a miniature football on to his lap.

"The Man U supporter is the fosterer, I suppose?" the inspector said.

Beverly opened her mouth to speak but suddenly decided not to say that it was Robbie holding the baby. She nodded, letting the inspector think what he wanted. A moment later she felt foolish; it was as if she had something to hide. The door opened then and a woman from Human Resources came in, walking briskly as though she'd hardly paused to open the door. Frank and Beverly looked behind her, expecting the third nurse to appear.

"I'm afraid Katherine Pickford won't be able to come and see you. She was on Iris ward this afternoon and I did phone through a message to say that I wanted to see her, but it seems that it wasn't passed on. She's off duty now. I've phoned her home but there's no answer. You could speak to her another day or I could give you her home address? You could try later?"

Frank coughed and turned to Beverly. Their eyes met, the look between them heavy with understanding.

"I think we'll take the address," he said, standing up, brushing down his clothes and straightening his tie. "We'll visit the lady at home, right, Beverly?"

Beverly nodded, her face thoughtful, her long nails tapping lightly on the cover of the photo album.

The letter changed everything. It was on the mat as Marilyn and Tina went into their house after their holiday. There was a lot of post but Marilyn flicked through the pile and found the envelope with Ray's handwriting on the front. *It's from Ray!* she said. Tina said she dropped everything and stood there in the hallway opening it and reading through the contents. Tina, not knowing what it was, struggled round her with the bags. After a couple of moments when her mum didn't speak she said she felt this heavy hand on her chest. Marilyn let the letter fall away and it floated on to the hall floor and stayed there in between the bags. Then she walked silently up the stairs and into her room.

Tina snatched up the paper and read the contents.

Ray had fallen in love with a woman and had moved down to Cornwall to live with her. She was in his surfing club, he said. She was twenty-five and he'd only got together with her *after* he and Marilyn split up. He was being as honest as he could because he wanted Marilyn to know the truth so that she could *move on*. He, himself, had already moved and was not leaving a forwarding address. It was with his solicitors, he said, so that they could arrange for the separation and so that, in time, when Marilyn sold the house, he could have his part of the money.

Tina told me all this the next day.

She wasn't able to tell her mum about the baby. I understood that.

Marilyn spent most of that first week back from holiday in her bedroom or slopping round the house in her nightclothes. Mostly she wouldn't eat, Tina said. She had moments, though, when she made an effort. She stood, in her pyjama bottoms and T-shirt, cooking a huge plate of chips or an omelette, talking enthusiastically about how hungry she was. Once it was on a plate in front of her she couldn't eat it. Most of it got chucked in the bin.

I popped in every day at some point. Once, I found Tina was crying. She showed me an email from Ray.

Dear Tina, Mum will have the letter by now. Don't think too badly of me. It's better for all of us – you as well – if I disappear off the scene. Love Ray.

I couldn't help but glance down to Ray's signature line, **Surfers Do It On Board**!!! How out of place it seemed. How mocking.

It made me think that Marilyn hadn't been the only one to lose Ray. He was Tina's stepdad even if she didn't think of him like that. I knew they'd been close. It was he who bought Tina the computer and showed her how to use it. *He was going to teach me to surf as well*, she'd told me once, laughing at the thought of it.

I didn't have the heart to remind her about the pregnancy. I phoned Kath on my mobile and told her what had happened. *Give them a while to adjust. Another week isn't going to make much difference*, Kath said.

On my way home from work one day I dropped by and found Marilyn cooking risotto. They'd been back almost a week and Marilyn looked a little wild, her hair pulled back in a ponytail with bits escaping round her face, an old cardigan hanging open over some shorts. On her feet were some high-heeled mules.

"Want some, Julie?" she said, giving me a heavy smile.

"No thanks," I said.

Tina walked slowly round the kitchen table to get the plates out of the cupboard. Behind Marilyn's back Tina made a thumbs-up sign to me, implying

153

that her mum was OK. It didn't look that way from where I was sitting. Marilyn was stirring the food round and round without stopping, her head bent over the pot, wisps of hair hovering unhygienically.

Tina sat down with a mound of rice and vegetables on a plate in front of her. Marilyn had a smaller portion.

"This is good," Marilyn said, lightheartedly.

"Um," Tina said, raising her eyebrows at me, in a hopeful way.

Marilyn took a couple of spoonfuls but ate woodenly. Then she placed one elbow on the table and her mood seemed to plummet. She rested her forehead on the cup of her hand and with her other hand tried to smooth her hair back.

"I can't," she said, "I can't. . ."

Tina put her own fork down.

"You must think I am completely barmy," she said, turning to me.

I was perplexed. What could I say?

"Don't be silly, Marilyn. You're just going through a bad—"

"How can I eat with this bloody hair in the way?" she said, her words cutting across mine. She stood up and walked out of the room. A second later we heard her running up the stairs and her room door slam. Tina and I were left sitting in front of the uneaten food. After a few moments I broke the silence.

"Shall I go home?"

"No, stay. I'll clear this up and we can go upstairs to my room," Tina said, standing up and lifting her plate over to the bin. She scraped her food away, the heat still rising off it. There was no sound from upstairs.

"She'll get through this," I said, with more certainty than I felt.

"She'll have to," Tina said, with her back against the work surface, her hand resting on her bump. Never had she looked so obviously pregnant. How could Marilyn fail to notice? She saw me looking at her and she rubbed her hand across her stomach.

"What a mess," she said.

Just then we heard heavy footsteps coming downstairs. We both tensed. The kitchen door swung open and Marilyn breezed in. Tina's mouth went slack and I found myself sucking air in through my teeth.

Marilyn had cut her hair off. She must have taken the scissors and clipped off her ponytail.

"That's better," she said, sitting down at the food again.

Her hair was jaw length, shorter at the back than the front. It looked choppy and strange, Marilyn's face thin and pale underneath.

"Come on, Tine, eat up!" she said, her words loud. She hadn't even noticed that Tina's plate wasn't there.

"I wasn't hungry," Tina said, walking past her out of the room. I stood up to follow but Marilyn reached out and touched me on the arm.

"Might be for the best," she said, a forkful of rice in mid-air. "Tina's been putting a few pounds on lately. She's probably worrying about me."

Her hand was shaking and the tears came. I sat back down again.

"Marilyn, it's none of my business but you're better off without him."

"I know," she said. "I really do know that now."

I sat very still while Marilyn cried.

How could Tina tell her mum about the baby? I understood completely.

I stayed away for a few days after that. I wanted to let them sort it out between them. *It's not my problem*, I kept telling myself. I took some extra shifts on at work which meant that I got back late at night with Mum in the car so I didn't call in to see Tina. Me and Mum went shopping a couple of times and I also went out with Kath, to the cinema and for a pizza. She wanted to know all the news and for a while I let everything out: Tina's secret, her fears, my worries. I didn't have to pretend everything was all right.

A couple of days later, coming home from a trip to the supermarket, I found Marilyn in my house talking to my mum. It was almost two weeks since they had returned from their holiday and there was a transformation. Marilyn looked good. She'd been to a hairdresser's and had her hair restyled. The short cut took years off her. She still had a lot of make-up on but she was wearing casual clothes, trousers and a blouse, and didn't look so tarty. On the table were some papers from estate agents.

"Hi," Marilyn said, as I went in. "What do you think of the makeover?"

"Great," I said, glancing down at the sheets. They were from an estate agent in Newcastle.

After she went home my mum told me that Marilyn had decided that she and Tina would move up north to get away from her bad memories and also be near her sister.

"Tina is going too?" I said.

"Of course. Mind you, it'll be months before they move. You know how long it takes to buy and sell property. You'll miss her, I expect. The two of you have got close. You can always visit!"

Tina and her mum were going to leave. It gave me an odd feeling. I went across to see her as soon as I could. She took me up to her bedroom and sat down in front of the computer. The window was open, the net curtain billowing in the light breeze. The room seemed calm. From another room I could hear a distant radio.

"Mum's in the shower," she said.

"You're moving," I said, in a mildly petulant voice. "Thanks for telling me."

"It's Mum's idea. I don't know if it will really happen. The main thing is that she feels better because she's made a plan *and* she's always happy when she's with my aunt. It'll get her away from here and her memories."

"And you'll go and live up there?" I said, disconcerted at her lack of emotion. We hadn't been friends long but I expected to see her slightly dismayed.

"If it happens. This week it's a good idea. Next week she might change her mind. Who knows?"

"She's actually looking for a new house. That means this house will have to be put up for sale."

"Not for weeks. The summer is a bad time for selling houses. The estate agent told my mum. I'm just glad she's going away for a bit. I want her to be with my aunt. My aunt can look after her."

"Who's going to look after you?" I said, and lowered my voice. "And the baby?"

"I can't think about that now. One problem at a time. I want to get my mum sorted out, then I'll worry about this."

Tina pointed to her stomach, hidden behind the folds of a loose shirt.

"I'm just taking it day by day. When Mum comes back from her sister's I'll sit her down and talk to her about everything."

The next day I watched out of my front room window as Marilyn pulled a small suitcase on wheels towards a waiting taxi. Tina stood in the front porch and waved. Then she went back indoors. Marilyn drove off with a new hairdo and plans for a new life. And she didn't have a clue about Tina and the baby.

CHAPTER EIGHTEEN

Marilyn phoned and said that she was going to be staying with her sister for a couple of weeks. She asked Tina to go up to Newcastle and help her look at new houses. Tina made excuses. She said the estate agent had rung and was sending a number of people to look at their house. Mostly she said she'd rather stay behind to spend time with me; seeing as, in a few months, she was going to move to a different part of the country.

Tina was relieved because her mum was somewhere else. I was still agitated. Another two weeks and Tina would be almost full term.

"You have to see a doctor," I said.

"I'm fine," she said, "I just need a break from worry and decisions for a few days. Now that Mum's out of the way I've got no pressure on me. I feel good, the baby's moving all the time. I've read it up on the internet. There's no bad signs at all. I need time to think. To decide what I'm going to do."

I was worried. Kath texted me every day. *Do U want me 2 talk 2 her? She needs 2 C a doc! Wot about the baby???*

"You can't just drift on like this," I persevered, after another few days had slid by. "You have to make arrangements for the birth of the baby. You have to think about what's going to happen afterwards."

I was beginning to hate the sound of my own voice.

"I have," she said, calmly.

We were in her kitchen sitting either side of the table. In between there was a book she'd ordered on the internet about pregnancy. The faces of a couple of babies stared up at us: big blue eyes and milky skin, wisps of hair and long eyelashes; one had a fist at its mouth, another had rosebud lips, puffed out and chunky.

"I'm going to have it adopted."

"Oh."

My mouth felt dry and I found myself licking the inside of my lips.

"It's for the best all round," she said, firmly.

"And the arrangements for the birth?" I said, after a few moments. "You'll have to contact social services. About the adoption?"

Tina turned her head away from me, her eyes fixed on the window.

"You must be thirty-five or thirty-six weeks now," I said, an edge in my voice.

"Still a long time to go," she said, dreamily.

"I can't deal with this any more! You have to tell someone!"

She rounded on me suddenly.

"Julia, this is not your business, right? I am the one who is pregnant. I'll make my own decisions and if it's getting you down then don't come over. I don't ask you to come round every day. Don't. Just stay away!"

Her face was hard, her eyes glittering. I'd never seen her like it before.

"I thought you liked me coming over," I said, weakly.

"I do. I did. It's just that you keep going on and on and on. I just don't want to hear it!" she said, gesturing with her hands as if to cover her ears.

"I won't come then!"

"Don't. And don't *worry* about me, I'll look after myself."

I walked out of her bedroom and down the stairs. I half expected to hear her voice calling me back but she didn't. I was astonished. In all the months we'd been friends I'd never seen her angry. Not once. I closed her front door firmly and walked across the street. I was due at work and quickened my pace. Once inside my house I slammed the door and stormed upstairs. I got my clean uniform out and threw it into my bag and zipped it up with force. Now she was on her own, see if I cared! Let her manage by herself. She obviously didn't need me.

But on my way back from work I knocked on her door. It took her ages to open it and when she did she stepped forward and gave me a hug. I stood rigid for a moment feeling awkward, then I put my arms round her. She felt hot and bothered.

"Sorry," she said.

"I brought some garlic bread from work," I said, with forced cheer.

We went on like that for a few days and I avoided talking about doctors. After the row she seemed more detached than ever. I talked to Kath about it over the phone.

"You should tell her that I know," she said. "Let me come and see her. Maybe I'll be able to get her organized."

She was right, I knew. I made the decision to get Kath involved. She could fob me off but Kath was an *adult*. She held a position of responsibility. She would have to take her advice. The next day when I arrived at Tina's house, carrying the bag of shopping she'd asked me to get, she was more talkative than usual. She'd done housework and the kitchen was pristine.

"I've made some plans," she said, in a casual voice.

I sat down, leaving the unpacked shopping sitting on the table between us. I glanced at my watch. I'd arranged for Kath to come in half an hour.

"I heard from my aunt Sheila last night. Mum's been up and down, she says. She's kept her busy, though, and they've found a couple of houses that Mum likes. Sheila says Mum should stay up there a bit longer."

I straightened up and began to line up the jars of pasta sauce and the yoghurts.

"Is that good?" I said. "Don't you think it would be better if she was here, when the time comes for the baby?"

"I don't need her here," Tina said, her voice strong and firm. "And it means that I don't have to tell her about the baby."

"Not straight away, you mean?"

"Not at all," she said, tapping her nails on the table.

"I don't get it," I said, undoing a plastic bag and removing a hand of bananas.

"Sheila says she's taken her to the local colleges. She might start a course. Thing is, Mum could actually stay up there and I could stay here until the house is sold. I could pack everything up. She doesn't need to come back at all."

"She'll know about the baby, though. At some point?"

There was impatience in my voice

"She doesn't need to know about it *ever*. I'll have it when she's not here," Tina said and stood up, making the chair and table rattle. She was shaking slightly. She seemed *charged* with something. I laid the bananas down and sat back. I wondered if she was going a bit strange, a bit loopy with the worry of it all. I glanced at my watch. Kath would knock on the door soon.

"She will find out, Tina. There'll be doctors and hospitals. There'll be health checks. There'll have to be social workers involved if you're going to give the baby up for adoption. She'll know. She's not an idiot, she'll find out."

"That's just it." She leaned forward, her hands on the table. "I've thought it all out. In another three or four weeks I'll be ready to give birth. I'm not even sure my dates are right. I could be further on than I think. If Mum is away when I have the baby there's no reason why she should *ever know*. As soon as I start my contractions I'll go to a hospital away from here. I'll get a cab and go to Accident and Emergency and tell them I'm on holiday, from outside London, and I've started sooner than I thought. Then, when the baby's born, I'll just get my clothes and leave. All they'll have is a false name. The baby'll be in a hospital, the best place for it, and I'll be home again. No one will ever know!"

The shopping sat on the table at odd angles. I tidied some of it up. I opened my mouth to speak but nothing came out. Tina was walking up and down, a hand on one hip, her stomach pushed out. No one could look at Tina and not know that she was pregnant. No one.

"Except for you and me," Tina said, excitedly. "We're the only ones who know."

The doorbell rang. I looked at my watch. Kath was right on time.

"There's someone else who knows," I said.

Later, I sat in Kath's car in the McDonald's car park. We had the windows open but it was still hot. My lap was warm from the bag that held my food. I had a chicken sandwich but I hadn't opened it. I was just mindlessly picking out the fries and dipping them into the ketchup before slotting them into my mouth. Kath's drink was on the dashboard and she reached for it and then seemed to change her mind.

"I know her mum's fragile, but honestly, why is she so adamant that she doesn't want her to find out?" she said.

I shrugged my shoulders.

"She didn't seem to mind too much. That you'd told me, I mean." She picked her drink up and made a noise sucking the milkshake up through the straw.

That had been a surprise. I'd thought Tina would see it as a sort of betrayal but she just accepted it in that soft, easygoing way that she'd developed. When Kath had gone through the medical facts and tried to persuade her to go to the doctor's she'd listened, but shook her head. When Kath tried to press the argument, she sat with her eyelids shut and her fingers on her temples as though she was about to meditate. This had worried Kath and she stopped and just started to ask her about her condition. Then Tina had explained her plan again. She gave every detail, even the cab firm that she was going to call and the false name she had chosen to give the hospital.

After a while Kath stood up to go and I went with her. I gave Tina a hug and said I'd be round the next day.

"I was surprised that you didn't, you know, *insist* that she went to a doctor's," I said.

"Mm. . ." Kath said, opening up her polystyrene box and easing out her Big Mac. "We've been doing some stuff on Psychology over the last few weeks and I've read up some fascinating case studies on teenage girls and pregnancy. I think that Tina was in a state of shock about this pregnancy. Her mum's problems allowed her to deny that the pregnancy was there. Now that her mum's out of the way she can no longer do that, so she's making plans to dispose of the baby as quickly as possible. That's another form of denial. I think if I pushed her she might well just give birth and give it away. And you know she'd regret that for the rest of her life. There are so many tragic stories of teen mums who gave up their babies and then spent years trying to trace them. I think we should play it softly softly. Go along with her. She's got four weeks to go, after all. Lots of things could happen. Her mum might come back. She may change her mind. She might just wake up one day and say, *I'm keeping it*. There's no telling what might happen. If we push her now then she may make a decision that she might not be able to back out of."

It made sense. I pulled out the box that held my chicken sandwich.

"We just wait and hope she changes her mind?"

"Absolutely," Kath said.

I went to bite into my sandwich but hesitated. I couldn't face it so I put it back into the box.

"We've got four weeks, after all. Maybe more if she goes over the time."

I collected the rubbish together, got out of the car and dumped it into a bin. Kath was probably right. In four weeks things might look a lot different.

We didn't have four weeks, though. The baby came four days later.

CHAPTER NINETEEN

I noticed the text message early in the morning. I woke about six and couldn't get back to sleep. My mobile was on my bedside table and I tutted when I saw it. I'd been so tired after my shift the night before that I'd forgotten to put it on to charge overnight. I sat up and looked at the screen to see that I had a message. I picked it up. It was from Tina. *Come over asap. Tina.* I looked at the time the message was sent. 03:57am.

I rang her immediately, pulling my jeans on at the same time.

"What's happened?" I said.

"It's started."

Her voice was a whisper.

"I'm coming over," I said, and ended the call.

An odd feeling was flickering inside me. I dragged the rest of my clothes on, not bothering to lace up my trainers. I stood for a minute to collect my thoughts. The baby was starting, that was what she meant. *The baby*. I picked up my bag and my mobile and found myself walking up and down the room a few times. I was nervous, no more than that. I was anxious, maybe even a bit excited. I made myself breathe slowly. I closed my bedroom door over and crept out, careful not to wake Mum up. I left a Post-it on the hall mirror. **Had to pop out early. Luv J.**

The street was quiet, no people and no cars moving. In the distance I could hear the wheels of something heavy and slow, like a lorry or a dustcart. I almost tiptoed across the street, and then noticed that Tina's front door was ajar. I walked in and closed it behind me. The hall light was on but she wasn't there. Then I heard a groan from the living room. I walked in and saw her lying sideways on the settee, her knees up to her chest, her face pushed into the pillow.

"Tina!" I said, with alarm.

She put her hand out and I grabbed it. She was breathing deeply, her whole body curled up into a knot. I knelt down and put my other hand on the back of her head.

"I'm calling an ambulance," I said, panic in my voice.

She shook her head furiously and gripped my hand in hers. Then, in seconds, she seemed to slump on the sofa, her knees dropping, the tension draining out of her. She turned her face towards me.

"It's a contraction," she gasped. "It's better now."

"You should be in hospital," I said. "You said, when it happened, you said you would get a cab and go to a hospital!"

"I didn't expect it so soon. I thought I had weeks to go."

She pulled herself up into a sitting position.

"I've been ill. I thought it was food poisoning. I was in and out of the loo. Then I went to bed and woke up in the middle of the night. The bed was wet. I thought for one awful minute I'd wet myself. I had a shower. I was changing the sheets and then these pains started."

"Your waters broke."

I'd read stuff about childbirth, just like she had. I knew about the waters breaking and how it meant that the baby was on its way. Then there were the contractions, the neck of the womb (*medical term, cervix*) opening up to allow the baby to move through. It all sounded so logical and so smooth.

"I didn't realize at the time. I tried to get dressed, to get a cab, but I couldn't. Every time the pains came I thought the baby was coming. I had to lie down."

She looked better, much better than she had moments before. She was sitting up breathing steadily, straightening the dressing gown that she had on. She needed to go to a hospital, I knew that. I sat beside her.

171

"I know that the baby isn't coming yet. I know that contractions can last hours but when it comes it's so . . . so painful I just can't imagine it getting any worse."

"Tina, let's call a cab and go to the hospital. We can't mess around here. You can get painkillers in the hospital. Face it, the baby's coming."

She shook her head even as I was speaking.

"Ring Kath," she said. "Tell her to come over. Please."

It was the next thing I was going to say. Kath had more authority than me. I let the mobile ring six or seven times and stopped. I left it a few seconds and rang again. This time I let it ring on. Eventually, a sleepy voice answered.

"Kath, it's Julia. Come to Tina's house. I think she's started."

"What? Get a cab, Julia. Get her to hospital."

"I can't. Her waters have broken. She's having contractions and in any case she won't. You've got to come. She'll listen to you."

The line went dead and I imagined Kath getting out from under the covers and stumbling to the bathroom to get dressed.

"Shall I make some tea?" I said, looking forlornly in the direction of the kitchen.

Tina didn't answer. She tensed up.

"It's coming again," she said, and lay sideways.

I watched her close her eyes and cradle her stomach.

"Aren't you supposed to breathe or something?" I said, helplessly.

She nodded and I saw her sucking breaths in through her mouth. Her knees rose up and she was in a ball again. She looked as tight as a spring.

"You need to relax," I said, standing up, stepping back, not really wanting to be there.

She didn't speak, just lay, her face creased up, a low sound coming from her. I looked around stupidly. What was I supposed to do? I knew that these contractions could go on for ages. I'd even heard of people being in labour for twenty-four hours or more.

"How long is it since the last one?" I said.

I looked at my wrist but I had no watch. I pressed my mobile and the screen lit up. I hadn't been there more than ten minutes. She'd been in the middle of one when I got there. What was it? Five minutes since the last one?

I knelt in front of her and rubbed at her shoulders but her muscles were plaited up. How long would it take for Kath to get here?

"You've got to relax."

I used a whispery voice, as calm and soothing as I could. She just let out a low howl, though, and seemed to become smaller on the settee.

"Think of other things," I said, weakly.

What was I talking about? Everything I knew about childbirth came from a web site and looked much easier in black and white print. *You will experience painful contractions but breathing exercises and positive thinking will ease these.* Or it came from television drama where women screamed and howled and men looked seasick and worried. There was always a doctor or a midwife around and nice machines that beeped quietly around the bed.

"Can you feel the baby moving?" I said, in some vague hope that the baby would help itself.

All I got from Tina was a half sob as she gripped on to my arm. Her fingers were digging into my skin but I didn't say a word. *How long's Kath going to be?* I thought, wildly, boring my eyes into the door and willing it to swing open and for her to march into the room and get things organized. I felt Tina's grip loosen and looked to see her lying back, her legs uncurling, her face as pale as wax, her expression one of disbelief.

"This is bad," she said. "It must be nearly time."

"How long have they been this painful?"

"For hours. I think," she said.

"Kath'll be here in a minute. She'll know what to do," I said, disengaging her hand from my arm.

I went out into the hall and opened the front door. I stepped out and looked up the street and then down the other way. I caught sight of my own house. There was no sign of any movement. After a late night my mum would probably sleep till gone eight. A car went by, driving slowly, almost coming to a halt every time it crossed a hump in the road. It wasn't Kath's. *Where is she?* I thought, a mild feeling of hysteria rising up in my stomach. It was one thing rubbing Tina's shoulders but something else entirely to help her give birth to a baby there on her living-room floor. The very thought of it made me feel lightheaded.

"Julia," I heard her shout, and bit into my lip.

When I went back in the room she was doubled up again.

"I'm going to call an ambulance!" I said, my voice cracking.

"No! No," she said and started to cry openly as she sat upright and pulled her knees up to her chest. Her mouth was set in a grimace and she held her hand out to me. I grabbed her fingers and she closed her eyes and sat rigid. She was making it worse for herself, I was sure. If she could just relax. She let out a wail, though, and I thought I was going to cry.

"Breathe, breathe," I said, pathetically.

I sat beside her and put my arm round her shoulder. This contraction was only a minute or two since the last one. Kath would want to know that. I had to keep my head and tell her and then she would disregard Tina's cries and get an ambulance. After a few seconds I felt Tina's breathing becoming more regular, her shoulders sloping. Her head lifted up from her chest. Her mouth was open and she looked dazed. Then, from outside, I heard the sound of a car door slamming.

"That'll be Kath," I whispered, a feeling of relief making me pat Tina's shoulder as though she was a little kid.

"I need to go to the toilet," she said, lifting herself off the chair, her face calm.

I held her arm until she got to the bottom stair and then I went out of the front door to see Kath. I groaned when I realized that it wasn't her. Only a red car that had parked further up. I looked back into the hall. Tina was halfway up the stairs. I crept back in and picked up her phone handset. If Kath didn't arrive by the time I'd counted ten I was ringing for an ambulance. I held the phone and counted slowly. I felt better because I'd made a decision. Once I'd got to ten Tina couldn't stop me pressing 999. I got as far as eight and Kath's car came out of nowhere, storming down the street, pulling up untidily a few metres down from where I was standing. She slammed her car door and aimed her keys at it as she was walking. The locks made a thunk sound and then she was in front of me.

"Where is she?"

"She's gone to the toilet. You've got to do something. It's awful! She's in the most dreadful pain."

I found that I was crying as I was speaking.

"The contractions are coming every couple of minutes, maybe even less."

Kath was walking briskly up the stairs. When she got to the top she said, "Tina, don't go to the toilet. Tina, don't sit on the toilet!"

We were both outside the bathroom door. Kath tried the handle. It was locked. She rattled it a few times and then looked around in a distracted way.

"Tina, unlock this door."

There was a shuffling sound and then the bolt slid back. Kath pushed the door open gingerly but it only opened a few centimetres. It wouldn't go any further.

"Oh no! Tina, move a bit so that I can get in!"

I could only see a little over Kath's shoulder. Tina was there, on the floor and there wasn't enough room for Kath to slide in. An awful howling sound came out of the room and I began to feel faint.

"Just move over a bit, Tina, so that I can get in!"

Tina edged herself along the floor so that she was face up to the bath panel.

"I want to push," she said. "The baby's coming!"

"Oh no." Kath stepped across Tina and turned the tap on at the washbasin. Tina was hunched up again, groaning into the floor tiles.

"Shall I get something? Hot water? What shall I do?"

"Phone an ambulance!" Kath said, opening and shutting cupboard doors.

"NO!"

The word seemed to gargle in Tina's throat. Then she turned round and tried to raise herself off the ground. "No, no, no."

"Don't upset yourself," Kath said, bending down, kneeling in the tiny space available. "Leave it, Julia, just get me a load of towels. There don't seem to be any clean in here."

I turned away, looking here and there around the landing until I focused on the airing cupboard. I grabbed a pile of towels and took them back to the bathroom. Kath was scrubbing her hands and arms with soap, the steam rising from the hot water tap.

"Get me some pillows so that I can wedge Tina up. There's no time to move her, hurry up!"

I went into Tina's room. Her bedding was on the floor and her mattress was wet. I looked away in dismay. It wasn't like this in films. I picked up the pillows and as I went back towards the bathroom I heard a shout of distress and Kath's voice, soft and firm.

"OK, this is when you start to push. When you feel the contraction coming you push. When it stops you stop. When I can see the baby's head I'll tell you to pant. Just do everything I say, OK?"

There was no time for me to put the pillows behind her. I just dropped them and went into the bathroom. Tina was partially on her side, Kath kneeling between her legs. I looked away with embarrassment. I edged round them and went and squatted by Tina's shoulders and head.

"Get a flannel and wet it. Keep her cool."

I did what Kath said and just then Tina screwed her face up and let out a grunt. I knelt down and put the wet flannel on her forehead but she pushed it away and grunted again.

"Pant, pant," Kath said, her face tight with concentration. "Pant!"

There was a moment's quiet when everything seemed to freeze and then Kath's face loosened up, her mouth opening with awe.

"Gimme a clean towel, quick!"

I reached for the towel and passed it to Kath. I turned back to Tina and heard a sound. A whimper. At first I thought it was Tina, moaning, crying with pain, but then the sound changed to a vigorous squeal. The baby. I swung round to see it in Kath's hands. A tiny purple baby, its face screwed up, its skin slimy and in places bloody. For a second its tiny arms moved, its hands in fists. It looked angry. It certainly sounded angry. It was a boy, I could see that much.

Kath was wrapping him in a towel, covering his rawness, leaving only a tiny V to see his face, a spray of dark hair on the top of his head. He was still crying, not so much a sob as a pitiful wail, as though he hadn't wanted to pop out into the world at all.

"Look, Tina," Kath said, holding him up. "It's a fantastic little boy."

But Tina just pushed her head into the floor, her shoulders rounded, her hair loose and covering her face.

Tina's baby had been born.

TWENTY

CHAPTER

Kath was attempting to clean the baby up, using a towel to keep it warm. Its legs and arms were moving about and every few moments it gave a cry that set my nerves on edge. Kath was looking stressed, getting up and leaning across to the washbasin to rinse her hands every few minutes, then squatting down and looking at the baby as if she didn't know where to start.

"What's the baby going to wear?" I said, stupidly, as if that was an important issue.

"Go downstairs," Kath said, as if she was pulling herself together and in charge again. "Find me some scissors. Boil them up in a pot. I'll have to cut the cord."

I couldn't move, my eyes were glued to the baby.

"Julia, this is important, hurry up."

"Shall I call a doctor?" I said, in a loud whisper as though Tina wasn't lying there on the floor beside me.

Tina shook her head vehemently and Kath looked pained and shrugged her shoulders. I stepped across Tina and went out of the bathroom. I was glad to go. In the kitchen I rattled round and found a couple of pairs of scissors in a drawer so I put them both in a pot and let them boil. All the while I was edgy, looking out through the kitchen window into the back garden, as if I had done something wrong and was waiting for someone to come and find me out. I took the scissors upstairs and heard Kath's voice going on about hospitals and aftercare and how the baby needed to be checked over. There was no answer from Tina.

I handed the pot with the scissors to Kath and mouthed the words *What's happening?* She shook her head in a kind of hopeless way and I backed out of the room while Kath got ready to cut the cord between the baby and the afterbirth. The very thought of it made me shiver, even though I knew it was the right thing to do and that it wouldn't hurt the baby in any way. Kath was also trying to clean Tina up and I thought it would be better for both of them if I was somewhere else. What would I have done if Kath hadn't been there? What kind of mess would I have made of it all?

I went into Tina's room and managed, with some difficulty, to turn her mattress over. I found some sheets in the airing cupboard and made the bed up and then tidied the room. Her bedside clock showed the time, 07:35am. I'd only been in her house for just over an hour. What an hour it had been. I was worried about it and at the same I was marvelling at what we'd done. What Tina had done. *A baby had been born.* After a chaotic start and a lot of panicking he'd arrived looking grumpy, as if he knew that he was entering a troubled household. Tina had lain on the cool tiles of the bathroom floor with Kath at one end and me at the other. It was a huge moment, when time seemed to pause and the baby sucked in its first breath and blew it back out in a cry that startled us all.

From where I was I could hear the baby's grizzly cry and Kath suggesting that Tina held him in her arms and maybe even tried to suckle him. There was no answer that I could hear and I just pictured Tina's head shaking vigorously, her arms crossing her chest. What was going to happen?

I went downstairs and made some tea, which kept me busy for a little while. As I did I heard movement from the bathroom and along the landing. When I carried the tray upstairs Tina was lying on her bed. The baby was rolled up in a towel perched on two pillows on the floor. He looked like a doll in a child's make-believe game. His dark hair was just fluff really, and looked as if it might fly off if somebody blew hard at him.

"Anyone fancy a cup of tea?" I said.

Kath nodded and I handed her a mug. I offered one to Tina but she shook her head. Not once did she look over at her baby. For a second I felt angry at her. The baby had stopped crying but I could hear the sound of him sucking his fingers greedily.

"Could you sort the bathroom out?" Kath said, taking a long drink of tea.

I nodded and went along the landing. The bathroom floor was in a mess. It was wet and there was blood. Over in the corner were some stained towels and a bin liner which held dark, bulbous stuff, that I didn't want to look at. The afterbirth (*medical name, the placenta; the lifeline, giving nutrients and sustenance to the growing baby*). What was I supposed to do with it? As I was mopping the floor up with the towels I kept looking over at it, a feeling of dread inside. What was to be done?

Kath came up behind me.

"I'm going out to get some things from the chemist down the road, nappies and baby milk."

"What if my mum sees you?" I said.

"I don't know. Hopefully she won't," Kath said, testily. "Tina needs to sleep it off. You keep your eye on the baby. Don't move far away from him. When I get back I'm going to contact her doctor. Leave that stuff." She pointed to the bag with the afterbirth. "It's clinical waste. I'll contact the hospital later and they'll tell me what to do with it."

"Does she know you're going to contact her doctor?"

Kath shook her head, "It doesn't matter. I've got to think of the baby. I'm hoping, if I don't rush it, give it a couple of hours, she'll come round. When I come back we'll feed the baby. Maybe, when she's got over the shock of the birth, she'll feel better enough that she'll take an interest in the little lad. These first few hours of bonding are so important."

She went out. I heard the front door click quietly behind her. Then I went into the bedroom and picked up the baby and sat in a chair. My arms felt shaky and my chest was trembling. There was this huge mass of emotion in my chest and I knew that at any minute I could burst into tears. He was an hour old and seemed to weigh almost nothing. I had him cradled in my arms, wrapped in a thick towel. Underneath he was naked; he didn't even have a nappy. His face was small with funny wrinkly skin. There were flaky patches near his ears and his lips looked dry. I could barely feel him breathing inside the towel and I had to look hard to make sure that he was.

Tina had her back to us so I gave him a hug and a couple of kisses on his forehead.

When Kath came back I went home for a while. My mum was walking sleepily around the kitchen and she gave a great yawn when she saw me.

185

"Was that Kath's car I saw pulling up?" she said.

I nodded.

"Yep. Tina's painting her bedroom and Kath and me are helping. That's why we made an early start."

The lie came easily.

"Toast?" she said.

I nodded. I was suddenly hungry. I ate three pieces of toast and then went up to the bathroom to splash my face and clean my teeth. In the mirror I caught sight of myself. I looked like someone who had been arrested and was having their mugshot taken. All I needed were some numbers at the bottom of the glass. I picked up the comb and pulled it roughly through my hair. Then I shouted bye to my mum and went back to Tina's.

There were raised voices coming from upstairs when I let myself in. It was just after nine-thirty. I rushed up and found Kath sitting at the end of Tina's bed with the baby on her lap. In her hand was a tiny bottle of milk. The teat was big but the bottle was small. Kath's hand all but covered it.

"You should try and feed this little boy. Even if you're going to have him adopted he still needs some love and care now," Kath told Tina, giving me a strained look.

"I can't," Tina said, holding the edge of the sheet up to her neck as if it was a napkin.

"Honestly, won't you even try? He's your little baby and he needs you!"

"I can't keep him."

"I'm not asking you to keep him, you've made that quite clear. Can't you at least take some *notice* of him?"

"I'll take him," I said. "You're tired, Kath. Why don't you have a shower? Tina won't mind. It's OK if Kath has a shower?"

I gave Kath a nod in the direction of the door. I thought I might be able to talk to Tina. She was my friend and she might take advice better from me.

"I won't have a shower," Kath said quietly, on the way out of Tina's room. "I'll go downstairs and see if there's anything to eat. It's twenty to ten now. Whatever she says I'm ringing her GP at ten o'clock."

"OK," I said.

I went back into the room and put the baby down on the pillows we had arranged. Somehow he had fallen asleep. Just like that. Moments earlier he'd been sucking at the miniature bottle. Now he was out for the count. I tucked his towel around him noticing the nappy that was on his bottom half, his legs sticking out, skinny and long, his feet pink and scaly-looking. I pulled my eyes away and went over to Tina's bed.

"Tina," I said, sitting down on the edge of the mattress. I took her hand and sandwiched it between mine, "I can't hold Kath back any longer. She's going to contact your doctor."

"She can't, Julia. She can't do that. You've got to stop her."

"But why? The baby's born. Look at him. He's lovely. Whatever you decide to do with him it's got to come out."

She shook her head.

"It'll destroy my mum."

"I think you're wrong. Your mum will rally round. She's a good person. I know she's been upset but she's been a good mum to you? Hasn't she?"

Tina nodded, her lips tightly shut, her eyes glassing over. Then she blinked and a tear slid down one of her cheeks.

"You've got to have faith in her. Just because she's had a bad time doesn't mean that she won't understand what's happened to you. If you do give the baby up for adoption you'll need her to support you. I think you underestimate her. She'll get over Ray and the divorce."

The crying got worse.

"What about if you talked to Ray? He was your stepdad, after all. He might have some advice. I could ring him if you want. Your mum doesn't need to know that you've talked to him."

She shook her head, wiping her face with the back of her hand, using the edge of the sheet to dry her eyes.

"You don't understand."

There were footsteps on the stairs and then I heard Kath's voice.

"It's five to ten, Julia," she called.

"I can't tell her, Julia. You have to help me. We could leave the baby somewhere. Outside a hospital or something. Where it'll be found."

She was losing the plot.

"It's a little *boy*, Tina. It's your son. You just can't take him out and leave him in the street. You can't do that!"

The door opened. I turned and saw Kath with the telephone receiver in her hand.

"Leave him where?" she demanded.

Tina took a deep breath. She sat upright and swung her legs out to the side.

"You've got to go, both of you. You've been really good, I can't tell you how grateful I am. I don't know how I would have managed on my own but you've got to go now. This is my problem. . ."

"It's not a problem," Kath said. "It's a baby."

"I want you to go – you too, Julia. You can leave me and the baby. I'll sort it out."

"We're not going anywhere, Tina," Kath said, holding the handset in her hand. "We're going to wait here for your doctor to come."

"No!" she said and moved slowly round the bed, clutching her nightie up to her stomach. "No, give me that." She put her hand out for the handset. "GIVE IT TO ME!"

Kath and I backed into the door, both shocked. She was becoming hysterical. A whimpering sound came from the pillows on the floor and I could see the baby moving, one of his doll-like feet sticking out of the towel.

"You're upsetting the baby," I said, softly.

"He's Ray's baby," she suddenly said. "Ray Hicks, my stepdad. That's who his father is. That's why I can't keep him and I can't ever tell my mum about him."

Nobody spoke. Tina stared at each of us in turn, then she stepped backwards and eased herself down on the bed. She seemed to deflate in front of our eyes, her mouth twisted up, her shoulders sagging, her arms limp. She glanced over at the baby for a second then looked back at us.

"You said Chris was his dad," I said.

"I lied."

"Ray Hicks. Your stepdad? You had sex with him?" Kath said.

Tina nodded.

The phone rang suddenly. It trilled impatiently in Kath's hand. We all looked at it. Tina leaned across and took it from Kath and answered it in a tiny voice.

"Hi Mum!" I heard her say.

I turned to check on the baby, all the while Tina's words in my head. *Ray Hicks, my stepdad.* I remembered his lime-green trainers and the signature line on his email *Surfers Do It On Board!!!*

"Yeah, a couple of people came but I haven't heard anything from the estate agent," Tina said, sitting up straight.

It was unreal. There was newborn baby on the floor and Tina was lying to her mum about real estate. I tried to catch Kath's eye but she was looking down at the carpet.

"Yeah, OK. That's fine. After the weekend, Monday or Tuesday," Tina said, her voice louder.

Kath had sat herself on the very corner of the bed, her head in her hands. Tina was sitting up straight, talking on the phone. The baby was moving about.

"Everything's fine here. I've just got Julia round and her cousin, Kath. We might . . . we might go shopping, later."

Ray wasn't her *real* dad. Tina had told me several times that she never thought about him like that. He lived with them, though. He married her mum. He bought Tina a computer and was going to teach her to surf.

"Bye Mum, look after yourself."

Tina let the receiver drop down.

"My mum sends her love to both of you," she said, huskily. "She's seen a perfect house and she's coming back down to London to see a solicitor."

"When?" I said.

"After the weekend. Monday or Tuesday. She's not exactly sure."

"Four days' time," I said.

The room was deadly quiet. Kath sighed. "What a mess."

"If my mum finds out about this. . ." Tina said, her voice cracking, her hands wringing at the end of her nightdress.

The baby made a sound and we all looked over at him.

Later that morning Kath had to go home and go to work. She took the afterbirth in a bag with her. She was going to leave work early, she said, and would try to get some clothes and stuff for the baby. She came back about four. That was when I went home, got ready for work and did a shift at the restaurant. I told my mum I was going to stay over at Tina's that night. Kath and me and Tina were going to have a girls' night in to celebrate the decorating.

The baby slept and fed and had to have its nappy changed several times. Kath did it and so did I. Tina wouldn't go near him.

Whenever we tried to raise the subject her face clouded over. Kath seemed resigned. I didn't know what to say so we ended up saying nothing. In the late afternoon Kath went out and bought a cardboard box, the type that people use to carry their pets in when they take them to the vets.

Tina slept in her room. Kath and I slept on duvets on the floor of Marilyn's bedroom. The baby slept in the middle of the bed flanked by two pillows. At half-past four the alarm on Kath's watch went and we got up, got everything packed and ready. Then we took the baby in Kath's car to a doctor's surgery that she knew. When no one was looking I took the baby in his box and left him, on the pavement, in a place where he could be easily seen. He never made a sound.

We drove round the corner and I watched until a police car pulled up. As soon as I knew that the baby had been found I got back in the car and drove off.

We'd done what Tina wanted us to do.

Beverly knew the street where the nurse lived. It was close to a park that she had played at when she was a young girl. The houses were old, three-storey buildings that had been converted into flats. Katherine Pickford's place was at the far end of the street, close to the entrance to the swing park. It was just after ten that evening when she and Frank Sullivan pulled into a parking space nearby.

After leaving the hospital Beverly had been called back to the office on an emergency. A boy had run away from his foster-carers and was making accusations of abuse. It was a delicate situation and Beverly had to find somewhere else for him to stay while the case was investigated. She could have done without this visit to the nurse but Frank Sullivan had been keen that they see the woman as soon as possible.

Neither Frank nor Beverly moved for a moment after Frank turned the engine off.

"How do we handle this?" he said.

"Gently. Whatever has happened here we have to tread carefully. This girl is obviously covering up for someone else and there has to be a good reason. Women don't give their babies away lightly."

Frank brushed at the front of his jacket and played with the knot of his tie. He didn't make any comment because he didn't want to get into a disagreement with Beverly. He had his views about what kind of woman would leave her baby in a box on the street. Someone who'd taken no precautions and allowed herself to get pregnant; someone who hadn't been able to face up to the responsibilities of motherhood; someone whose first concern was for themselves and not the baby.

"My guess is that it's a young girl. Someone a bit naïve perhaps, who didn't know she was pregnant until it was too late to get a termination."

Termination. The word offended him. How easy life was these days for the young and reckless. Get into trouble? Find some nice professional who'll get you out of it.

"Let's go," he said.

Outside the car it was quiet. A couple of teenagers were walking by, talking quietly, one of them staring down at the screen of a mobile phone. A dog started to bark somewhere in the distance and after a few moments another joined in. The sound of screeching wheels made him turn and look. Further down the street a car had come to a halt and was double parked, its passengers sitting waiting, the deep bass sound of music thudding along the road.

Frank could feel a headache coming on. He turned away and walked towards the house. Beverly was in front of him.

"Would you like me to ask the questions?" she said.

"If you don't mind," Frank said, patting his pockets to get his notebook out.

Beverly placed a long fingernail on the bell marked *K. Pickford*. After a few moments a voice sounded from a speaker on the wall.

"Yes?"

"I'm here to see Katherine Pickford? My name is Beverly Ward. I'm with Detective Inspector Sullivan. We wanted to talk to you about—"

The voice interrupted her. "Come upstairs, my flat's on the second floor."

There was a buzzing sound and Beverly pushed at the front door which swung back to show a narrow hallway with two bikes parked head to head along it. They edged past and walked up the stairs. Frank could hear the sound of a television set coming from the downstairs flat. Beverly, after a moment's search, had retrieved the book of photographs from her bag and was holding it in readiness. On the first-floor corridor they headed for an open door at the far end. A young, well-built woman with dark hair appeared in the doorway.

"Are you Katherine Pickford?" Beverly said, giving what she hoped was a reassuring smile.

"That's me," the young woman said.

"This is Inspector Sullivan—" Beverly started to say.

"Where have you been? It took you long enough to find me," Katherine Pickford said, impatiently.

Frank and Beverly looked at each other with surprise and followed the nurse into her flat.

CHAPTER TWENTY-ONE

It was the worst week I'd ever known.

After leaving the baby on the pavement and waiting until someone found him, we drove off through the early morning streets, both plunged into silence. We hadn't even given him a name. We just called him *Baby*.

Because it was still early the traffic was light, mostly lorries and vans and the odd bus. We made good time, passing by parades of shops, schools, industrial parks and office buildings until we came back to our own local area, street after street of terraced houses. Behind us we'd left a mystery. In front of us the day stretched ahead. What was there to talk about? Neither of us felt good about what we'd done. The atmosphere in the car was uncomfortable.

Kath dropped me off at Tina's. She drove too quickly up the street, bouncing over a speed hump. She didn't even pull in to the pavement to let me out, she just paused, leaving the engine idling, while I undid my seat belt.

"I'll come and see Tina tomorrow, just to check on her," she said.

"Have we done the right thing?" I said.

She shrugged and leaned her elbows on the steering wheel.

"What else could we do?"

I watched her go and felt terribly alone. I took Tina's keys out of my pocket, and went in. I found her sitting on the stairs. It looked like she'd been there for a while.

"Did you do it?" she said.

I nodded.

"Did you wait till someone came?"

I nodded again. I had no words.

"So it'll be all right," she said, and put her face into her hands.

When I first knew Tina she'd been strong and full of common sense. Now she looked like a middle-aged woman, her dressing gown badly tied up, her hair greasy and lopsided, her skin the colour of candle wax.

"He didn't cry though," she said. "Did he?"

"He didn't make a sound," I said and sat down on the stair below her.

Tina slept on and off all day. I left her late that night, in her mum's room, watching a tiny television set that was on a chest of drawers. The next day Kath came to check on her. She'd brought a bag with her with borrowed equipment in it. *I'm in a rush*, she said and checked Tina's temperature and pulse and blood pressure. Then she packed her stuff back into the bag and left it in the corner, telling us not to touch it. *I'll get the sack if anything happens to it*, she said in a snappy way. Tina just sat looking vague and far away; she hardly noticed Kath's mood. I followed Kath downstairs.

"I'm the one who'll get in trouble for all this," she hissed. "I'm the oldest. I'm a *nurse*. I should have known better!"

"You did what you thought was right," I said.

"It's all over the television. Someone will have seen us. You and Tina, you're youngsters. I'm meant to be the responsible one. I'll get the blame for this! I'll probably get chucked out of the hospital!"

She left, leaving the front door swinging open and I stood very still for a moment. Had we done the right thing? Had we?

I stayed until later in the day when I had to go to work. This pattern repeated itself over the next couple of days: Tina distant and childlike; Kath brusque and agitated. Me? I was in the middle, trying to keep Tina calm while at the same time reassure Kath. In between times I went to work.

The worst thing was the crying. It caught me unawares. I'd go into Tina's room and find her face down on the pillow shaking with sobs. Then, later, when she needed to go to the toilet, I found her slumped down on the floor, her face livid with crying. I knew she got upset when I wasn't there but what could I do? I phoned Kath to ask her. *She'll have to come to terms with it in her own way*, she said, dismissively. Then, after Tina had got up and got dressed I found her out in the front garden standing over the wheelie bin, wiping her face with the back of her hand. In the bin was the plastic wrapper that had held the nappies: *extra small*, *for newborns*.

I told Kath when she came round but she just shook her head in an irritated way. It was as if she'd lost any sympathy for Tina. I was worried about her. My big, generous, saintly cousin looked distracted. I noticed lines across her forehead and she didn't have such a rosiness about her skin. She seemed to chew at her lips, especially when she was taking Tina's blood pressure, or her temperature.

After a couple of days Tina seemed to rally round. She bathed, got dressed, washed her hair. She even tidied up her bedroom. Kath took all her medical stuff away and said she would be round in a couple of days. The front door closed behind her before I had a chance to say goodbye. It was as if Kath wanted to get away from us as quickly as possible.

Tina was sitting in the kitchen. She was drinking from a mug that had palm trees and surfboards on it. She saw me looking and gave a half smile. In a quiet voice I asked her about Ray Hicks. She answered calmly. She had completely lost that hysterical edge that she had in those hours after the baby had been born.

"Ray and me only did it once. It wasn't like some big love affair or anything like that. Trust me to get caught my first time."

I smiled at her attempt to be lighthearted.

"Did he . . . you know . . . make the first move?"

"Nah. I know it looks like that. Thirty-five-year-old bloke with his seventeen-year-old stepdaughter. But it wasn't. We were friends, me and him. I didn't think about him like my *dad*, or even a relative really. I was twelve when he first came round, thirteen when they got married. I know I took his surname, but that was more to please Mum. I liked him though. He spent a lot of time with me. We were friends. I could talk to him about anything."

"And was it . . . when he was still living here?"

She was quiet for a minute and then she nodded.

"You remember I told you my mum had gone to her sister's? So that she didn't have to see Ray moving his stuff out of the house? It was then, that

Saturday before Christmas. They'd been split up for over a month."

The Saturday before Christmas. I remembered that that was the day that I'd first had sex with Ben Holland. How long ago it seemed. A lifetime.

"Chris came round to visit. I hadn't seen him since he'd gone to university and he was so different. He'd lost all this weight and he looked at me so oddly. As if . . . as if I was the fattest person he'd ever seen!"

She was smiling but there was a hardness round her mouth.

"He'd changed. He hardly got in the front door when he dumped me. *We just haven't got anything in common any more.*"

"I was upset and I wasn't. Ray was packing upstairs and he made some joke about Chris going to do a degree in building Lego models. *What do you need him for?* he said. I helped him pack and he told me about the time when he was in uni down at Exeter. We sat talking for hours, even after all the packing was finished. With Mum not here everything seemed different. Like he wasn't a member of the family at all. He was leaving, going. My mum knew it. I knew it. It was like we were two people who'd just met."

"Didn't you think about what it would do to your mum?"

"No. . . Yes. . . I just got carried along with the

moment!" she said, an edge to her voice. "We had some wine. A lot of wine. We sat on the floor of the spare room, and it looked so different with all Ray's computers and stuff packed in boxes. It was like we were in a different house and one thing led to another. I can't even say who started it. I think he might have pulled back at one point and I kept on. I liked him. I was embarrassed about Chris dumping me like that. My mum was there, in my mind, but she was also far far away."

"What about afterwards. What did he say?"

"We both woke up early in the morning. I saw him standing at the bottom of the bed in the spare room. He was saying, *Shit, shit, shit*. Then he kept saying sorry. That he could hardly remember what we'd done, whether we'd actually *done It*. He was in a state. I said I couldn't remember, you know, just to make him feel better. But I knew we had. I remembered. When my mum turned up later that day I thought I was going to be sick."

"She never guessed?"

"You know what my mum's like. She was so focused on Ray, and whether she could get him to change his mind and stay, she hardly noticed me."

"And then he left."

Tina nodded, "And then I had a period and I thought, *That's it!* It was a terrible mistake but now it's over and Mum never needs to know."

She reached for the cup with the surfboards, hesitated and then pushed it away.

"What an idiot I was."

Kath rang me later.

"Have you seen the news reports?" she said.

"No," I said. I'd been avoiding them.

"They've got film of the car. Where we left the baby!"

"The registration number?"

"No! Just the car. A lorry pulled up beside us. It's only a matter of time before they find us."

What could I say? I was living from day to day. It was an unreal time. The gravity of what we'd done hadn't really hit me. We'd left a baby in the street but we'd done it for good reasons. Wasn't that acceptable?

"The police will turn up," Kath said.

"Don't worry so much," I said, tired of it all.

"Maybe it would be best all round if they did find us," she said, sounding resigned.

In the middle of the week the exam results arrived. I almost laughed.

"That's disappointing," my mum said when I told her. "Never mind, you can retake it, can't you?"

I nodded and my mum talked on about *more work* and *proper revision*. I took the slip and pinned it to the noticeboard in my room. Tina's envelope sat unopened on her hallway table. I offered it to her a couple of times but she just shook her head.

Four days after we left the baby outside the doctor's a change came over Tina. She began to talk about him non-stop.

"What will happen to him, to the baby, do you think?" she said.

We were in her room and she was sitting cross-legged on the floor in the middle of a pile of family photos. That day she appeared thinner, gaunt almost. I knew she wasn't eating properly. Kath had left an hour or so before, checking on her health, making sure her breasts were not leaking with milk. The whole thing had made me squirm and I'd made myself busy out in the hallway.

"Do you think he'll be adopted straight away?"

"I don't know," I said. "I'm sure it'll be soon. You hear about couples adopting newborn babies."

"What kind of people will adopt him?"

"Nice people. They have to be. They'll have been vetted."

"What name will they give him?"

"I don't know. Maybe he'll keep the name that the nurses gave him."

"Bobby?" she said.

She looked thoughtful and her lips were moving silently as though she was saying the name over and over, seeing how it fitted. Then she went back to her photos, making piles out of them, flicking through them as though they were playing cards.

"I'll have to go soon," I said, wondering when she was going to start being normal again, or if she was *ever* going to be like she was before.

"Before you left him. You did check that he was all right? That he wasn't crying. You definitely checked, didn't you?" she said.

"He wasn't crying," I said. "He was asleep."

"I just wondered," she said and went back to sorting out her photos.

Later I found her on her computer writing a letter. *Dear Bobby*, it started.

"What are you doing?" I demanded.

"Just writing a letter to Bobby," she said, as if he was a cousin she hadn't seen for a while.

"But you're not going to send it?" I said, incredulous.

"No, not now. Maybe when he's older. You know, if he ever comes to find me. Then I'll be able to show. . ."

But she couldn't go on. Her shoulders started to shake.

"Oh, Tina!" I said.

The sound of the front door slamming made us both sit up.

"Tine!"

"It's Mum!" Tina said, her face dropping.

"OK," I said. "Just act normal."

Marilyn Hicks had come back. Too late to be of any use to anybody.

TWENTY-TWO

CHAPTER

Marilyn had returned a day later than she'd said but she was bright and cheerful and full of news about a couple of *perfect* houses that she'd seen in a village just outside Newcastle. She gave Tina a hug and then her face creased up with concern.

"You don't look well, Tine," she said and looked over at me.

Tina told her she'd had food poisoning and had been laid up for a few days.

"And lost some weight, as well!" Marilyn said, cheerfully.

I made my excuses and left them together.

I spent the next couple of days away from Tina. I sent her a few texts and I got answers from her. Everything seemed to be all right. Marilyn had no idea of the drama that had taken place in her house and Tina's texts sounded positive, *normal* even. Being on my own, away from her, brought about a change in me, though. After days of being the sane, sensible one, I now found myself in a dark mood and on the edge of tears. I began to think about the baby that we'd left in a box by the side of the road. His name was Bobby, the newspapers said, and he was living in foster care while *awaiting developments*. That meant while they were trying to find his mother. I saw this picture in my head of an abandoned baby, lying precariously on the side of a motorway, the cars screaming past, the mother's back disappearing in the distance. It made me feel heavy a lot of the time, my legs and feet like lead. Or maybe it was just my period coming.

Marilyn came over to see my mum. I heard them talking in the kitchen, Marilyn's voice all high and girly and full of excitement. I listened at the door and heard her saying that she and Tina would have a brilliant time up in Newcastle. The shopping centres were huge and now that Tina had lost a bit of weight Marilyn was going to take her to a gym and get her toned.

It made me feel angry.

Exactly one week after we left the baby outside the doctor's I decided to go and tell her how I was feeling. I'd woken up with a headache and grumbled about it all morning. At midday I went across to her house and waited until Marilyn skipped down the stairs and opened the front door. She had a bag hooked over her shoulder and brought with her a cloud of perfume that made me blink a couple of times.

"Hi, Julie," she said.

"It's Julia," I said, exasperated. "My name's *Julia*, not Julie."

"Oh, silly me," she said, unperturbed. "Tina's just getting up, I think. I'm off out. You can wait for her in the kitchen. Make yourself a drink."

I filled the kettle up as the front door slammed behind Marilyn. The tea bags had run out so I looked in the cupboard for a new packet that I was sure I'd seen. I pulled it out and saw something wedged in behind. It was a box with a picture on the front of a baby bottle with a huge teat. The words *For newborns* were on the front. Kath had bought two. One of them she'd used but the other sat in its box unopened.

I sat down at the table and listened to the kettle boiling up. I held the plastic bottle in my fingers. It would only hold a tiny amount of milk. Just enough for a newborn baby's stomach.

The sound of Tina coming down the stairs made me look towards the door. The heavy pounding of her footsteps annoyed me.

"Hi," she said, coming into the kitchen.

I nodded to her, still clutching the bottle in my hand. She glanced past me, not noticing.

"Any tea?" she said.

"The kettle's just boiled."

She wasn't even dressed. It was twelve o'clock and she was just relaxing, looking after herself. I stood up.

"I'm going home," I said.

"Are you all right?" she said.

She was pouring hot water into a cup. She did look thinner, like the old Tina. Then the next second she looked just a stranger, somebody I didn't recognize.

"You OK?"

I didn't answer. I placed the baby bottle in the middle of the table.

"Where'd you find *that*?" she said, looking at the bottle.

I gestured to the cupboard.

"Oh. Thank goodness Mum didn't find it!"

There was relief in her voice and she was trying for a smile. I half expected her to wipe her forehead and say *Phew!* I closed my eyes and shook my head from side to side, my face rigid. When I looked at her again her expression had faded. Her hand was trembling, holding a teaspoon in mid-air, a tea bag hanging untidily over the side, dripping on to the floor.

"Is that all you think about? Whether or not Marilyn will find you out?"

"You know I don't."

"Don't you ever think about him? The baby?" I said.

She put the teaspoon down and leaned back against the sink.

"You know I do," she said. "But I have to try and put the whole situation out of my mind. I've made my decision."

"But he's your *son*," I said, softly. "Never mind how he came about."

"You know my reasons. I can't have my stepdad's baby. I can't."

"Never mind about you and your mum and your stepdad. Did you ever think about what's best for him? What sort of life he will have?"

"A good life with loving parents."

"But not his own mum. When he's old enough they'll sit down with him one day and tell him he was left in a box by the side of the motorway."

"*Motorway?*" she said, her voice high.

"Road, I mean," I said, shaking my head.

She rolled her eyes. As if she was being told off by some teacher. It enraged me suddenly.

"You go on and on about your mum. *I can't do this! I can't do that! What if my mum finds out?* But it's not about that, it's about you. You're just using your mum as an excuse! You knew for weeks that you were going to dump this baby. You strung me along and then Kath. You never had any intention of going to the hospital!"

"I never expected to start so soon."

"You wouldn't even look at the baby. Maybe it's not your mum you're trying to protect, maybe it's you!"

She put her fingers on her temples. I'd seen it before. It didn't stop me.

"You owe that baby something. Even if you're set on having him adopted you owe him an explanation. A history."

"What good would that do? What would it get from knowing me?"

"It's a baby, Tina. A boy. Not an *it*! Look. . ."

I picked up the bottle and held it up.

"This is all that's left," I said, my voice breaking.

He wasn't my baby, but I'd taken him from the car and left him by the side of the road. Tina shook her head in that dogged way she had, her eyes closed; that way she couldn't hear what was being said or see what was happening. In a moment of temper I threw the bottle down on to the floor and it bounced up high and fell, skittering across the surface into the corner of the room. Then I turned and walked out of her house.

I told myself it was for the last time.

Frank Sullivan stood up even though Katherine Pickford told him to *grab a chair*. Beverly sat down, her legs neatly crossed, the album of photographs sitting on her knee. The three of them were crowded into the kitchen of the small flat. On the table were the remains of a bottle of wine and a glass. From another room he could hear the soft thudding beat of music.

"My flatmate and her boyfriend. They've got the living room tonight!" Katherine said.

She pulled a chair out and sat down. She took a great sigh and then spoke.

"Am I going to get into trouble for this?" she said.

"What sort of trouble?" Frank said, warily.

There was the issue of whether a crime had been committed or not. The baby had been abandoned. He looked down at his notepad to collect his thoughts. His opinion was that there should be some sort of reprimand in such cases. It would never happen, though. The authorities always looked kindly on these situations. Women or girls who give birth to inconvenient babies were always given the benefit of the doubt.

"I don't know," Katherine said, using her fingers to push the plate of food away. "For not telling anyone.

For not getting in touch with the authorities. I am a nurse. . ."

"I can't say for sure. . ." Frank said.

Beverly butted in. "We are not here to apportion blame, Katherine. We are here to try and find the mother. It's been a week now and she may still be in need of some medical care."

Katherine shook her head. "I've looked after her the best I could."

"In any case, she may be suffering from depression. . ."

"Look," Katherine said, "you don't have to persuade me. I know who she is and I'll take you to her. Who do you think sent you the receipt for the clothes? I've been waiting days for you to get here. You have to know that we did what we thought was best. I just want to know if I'm going to be in trouble. If I might have to face a disciplinary hearing at the hospital or something."

"I can't comment on that. Whatever happens, the fact that you led us to find the baby's mother will help."

Frank shut his notebook and slid it into his inside pocket. There was no point in writing anything down.

"Her name is Tina Hicks. She's seventeen. She had no idea she was pregnant. Her mum's not very strong, you see, and there are problems about the father, but I probably shouldn't say any more. I'll get my jacket and take you to where she lives."

Frank's ring-tone sounded. It was a well-known tune; a football anthem which sounded out of place in the middle of such a discussion. He'd realized this on previous occasions, in the middle of serious interviews. He flipped the lid up and decided once and for all to change it.

"Sullivan," he said, and then listened quietly to the voice on the other end.

Beverly reached across the kitchen table and put her hand on the nurse's arm.

"These situations are always difficult. Young mothers who simply can't face what has happened. Believe me, it's better for her to face up to it now rather than live with the knowledge of it for the rest of her life. Because she'll never forget it."

Frank snapped his phone shut. Katherine and Beverly looked round at him.

"There's no need for you to take us to Tina Hicks," he said. "There's been a development."

After the row with Tina I had a long bath. As I soaked in the water I thought of Sara Dewey and that day that she'd come up to me in the shopping centre and told me that she and Ben Holland had finished. I'd been sure that she wanted to be friends again. At the time I'd dismissed it. Now I wondered if I'd done the right thing.

Sara had hurt me. When she went off with Ben my world shrank to nothing. For weeks I'd lived in a social bubble and it had taken Tina, a bookish, shy, overweight girl, to help me break out. We'd become close, maybe even closer than Sara and I had been. We'd certainly been through more. I'd seen Tina as a simple sort of person: a loyal friend, a good daughter, a girl of strong, sensible views. The last few weeks had turned that on its head and Tina seemed like a car that had gone out of control.

It frightened me. I didn't want to be a passenger any more.

I dried myself and then got dressed. I found my mobile and scrolled through my address book. Sara's name and number came up. I thought of ringing her. For a moment I saw myself in her kitchen, clasping a mug of tea, telling her the whole story. Sara would be opposite me, astonished by what had happened, her mouth open in a perfect O. I'd be a kind of celebrity; full of the details of Tina's disastrous life, a first-hand witness to the sensational events that had unfolded. When Sara and I had been friends she'd sneered at Tina and called her a *fat virgin*. How wrong she had been.

I dropped my mobile on the bed and sat down. How easy it would be to pick up the bits of my old life. Me and Sara; two look-alikes, hanging around together again. Like getting back on a bus that I'd left earlier. Sara and me; best friends again. Except that she never really was my best friend. How could she have been when she took my boyfriend away. Ben Holland – even though he hadn't been worth having, it still didn't make it right that she took him.

Tina was my friend.

I found myself walking up and down my room again. I was agitated. It was nine-fifteen but I had to go back and see her; I had to mend the row. I picked up my bag, pushed my mobile in and went out. The street was dark and quiet. In the air there was the faint smell of burning, the remains of a bonfire lit in a garden somewhere nearby. The night air had a chill in it and made me think of autumn just round the corner. I rubbed my arms and walked across to Tina's house and knocked on the door. From the window I could see a downstairs light. The hall light clicked on and the front door opened a moment or two later. Marilyn stood there. She rubbed her eyes as if she'd been dozing. Her new hairstyle was flattened down one side.

"She's upstairs, I think," Marilyn said, yawning.

"I'll go straight up," I said.

I walked slowly up the stairs, thinking about what I was going to say. I had to be calm. However bad I felt, Tina must feel ten times worse. I knocked lightly on her door. There was no answer.

"Tina," I called.

Was she asleep? I pushed the door open a few centimetres. The room was in complete darkness. I felt my shoulders droop. I had it in my mind that we would talk tonight, clear the air, be mates again. I hesitated, then walked a couple of steps into her room.

"Tina?" I said in a loud whisper.

There was no answer and I was about to turn away when I noticed that the bed was rumpled but flat. I turned the light on. Tina wasn't there. I tutted to myself and went back out into the hall. The bathroom door was shut but there was no sound. I knocked and turned the handle. It was empty. I stood for a moment, remembering the scene in there just a week ago. There was no sign that anything had happened. The floor was clean and the towels were hanging tidily over the rail. I shook my head. Where was Tina?

I walked downstairs and leaned into the living room.

"Tina's not upstairs," I said.

"Oh," Marilyn said, pointing the TV remote and lowering the volume. "Maybe she popped out to the shops when I was asleep?"

I nodded. "I'll go and look."

I walked along the street and round the corner to the small group of shops. The smell of chips was making me hungry but I resisted. Tina wasn't there, and neither was she in the sweet shop. The minicab place was empty except for a couple of the drivers who were sitting behind newspapers, waiting for a fare.

I went back to her house. Where would she go? She hadn't been out of the house since the birth and not much before then. Marilyn opened the door again.

"She's not there," I said.

"Maybe she's gone to see some other friends?" she said.

I gave a half nod. Tina didn't have any other close friends, and she wasn't likely to pop out to the pub to see some of the others from school after what she'd been through.

"Can I just get a couple of my things from her room?" I said, reluctant to go home.

But Marilyn had turned away and wandered off into the living room.

I went back upstairs and into her room, looking round as if there might be some answer there as to where she had gone. On the floor by her bed was her school bag. It reminded me of another time, when we walked to school together and worried about essays and grades. It was only seven or eight weeks before, but it seemed years back. So much had happened. I sat down on Tina's bed and wondered where she had gone. The pillows on the bed were askew so I leaned across and straightened them. Underneath one of them was the baby feeding bottle, the one that I had chucked on the floor earlier. Tina had retrieved it and had it here in her room, had been lying with it by her pillow.

How hard I had been.

I stood up. Where had she gone? I stepped across to the chest of drawers and saw a piece of paper that had been folded in four. My name was written on it, *Julia*, so I unfolded it.

Dear Julia, I'm so sorry. Love Tina.

I read it over and said it out loud. All the time a bad feeling was forming inside me like a ball of tangled string. I'd heard this line before. In a story that Tina had told me. *I'm sorry. . . I'm so sorry. . .*

I went downstairs. I stopped at the living-room door but couldn't go in to tell Marilyn. Instead I walked swiftly outside. The street was empty, not a soul in sight. I pulled Tina's door shut and half walked, half ran to the end of the road, turning into the next street. Some kids were hanging round on bikes.

"Have you seen a girl?" I said, breathlessly, hardly pausing long enough for them to give me their shrugged shoulders as an answer. How long ago had she written the note? It was hours since we'd had the argument. I didn't bother with the shops, I knew she wasn't there so I turned into the road that led towards the motorway. I crossed it, zigzagging between a couple of cars that were trying to squeeze past each other. I knew where she was going to be. I was sure. The same place as her mum headed for on Christmas Eve. *She tried to kill herself*, Tina had said. *I've never told anyone this but my mum tried to kill herself.* I had dismissed it. Tina was reading too much into it. She'd found her mum leaning on the rail, the traffic accelerating underneath her. What did that prove?

I ran along the next street, pausing to let a man and a big dog go past. Up ahead was the lane that led to the footbridge. I was running and puffing, my bag flying out behind me. When I got to the turning the noise of the traffic hit me. It was dark ahead, the footbridge lit up only by occasional lights. There was a figure, I was sure, in the middle somewhere. I called her name but it was drowned by the roar of the cars and lorries. At the edge of the footbridge I waved but she was side on, looking down at the road beneath her.

It was Tina. A feeling of dread hit me. She seemed to be leaning forward, her hair hanging loose.

"Tina!" I shouted, "Tina!"

I ran on and she suddenly turned and saw me. It was too dark to see her expression but I slowed down a bit, panting like mad.

"Are you all right?" I said, coming closer.

"I'm all right," she said: "Are you? You look like you've seen a ghost!"

She was smiling. She'd changed her clothes and looked more like her old self. She even had a bag with her, the tiny rucksack she used to carry with the teddy bear hanging off it.

"What are you doing here?" I said, leaning on the rail beside her, my heart pumping wildly from my run.

"Just thinking," she said and then her forehead wrinkled. "Why were you running?"

"I was just a bit worried. After the row and stuff. . ."

"Yeah, sorry about that. . ."

She was staring into the distance. I looked around. On one side of the motorway where the golf course was it was completely black. On the other there were rows and rows of lights coming from the houses and the streets.

"Hang on a minute," Tina said, leaning back. "You didn't run down here because you thought I was going to do something silly?"

"*No!*" I said.

She was looking straight at me.

"You did! Oh Julia, I would never do anything like that. Never!"

"I found the note in your room. I just thought. . ." I had a mix of feelings, relief and embarrassment. "The note. It was the same as your mum's. . ."

"I was saying sorry about the row. About everything. I am sorry. I've been an idiot. I was going to put the note through your letterbox but then I changed my mind. You thought it was a *suicide* note?"

"Not really," I said.

She turned and hugged me. She'd got some of her strength back because I could hardly breathe.

"You're the best, Julia. I couldn't have had a better friend than you all these weeks."

We stayed in the middle of the footbridge. I didn't feel cold any more and once I got used to the noise of the traffic it didn't seem so loud. The golden beams of the oncoming cars were mesmerizing, one after the other, like a stream of light running beneath us.

"I think about the baby all the time," Tina said. "I wonder what I would have called him, you know, if he'd stayed."

She made it sound as though he'd left of his own free will.

"Do you wish . . . do you think it would have been better if he'd stayed?" I said.

"I thought having the baby – telling my mum – would bring so many problems. But giving him away. . . It just created a whole new load of grief."

I could hear the sound of a police siren in the distance. It came closer and I watched as the blue flashing light zipped past underneath us and sped away up the road.

"This afternoon, after you left, I went back upstairs to bed. My mum came in about one and came running up the stairs. *Guess what?* she says. *The estate agents are sending two different couples round to look at the house.* She was beaming. Ray was right about being honest with her. By moving away and living with this other woman it made Mum face up to the truth. It's been painful but Mum really seems *stronger* now."

I didn't speak. I couldn't really work out what she was saying, where she was going with the conversation.

"If I tell her about the baby, won't it just throw her back into depression?"

"Or maybe it'll make her stronger still?"

I didn't really know. How could anyone know how Marilyn would take the news?

"I wouldn't have called him *Bobby*," Tina said, after a while. "I would have called him *Jack*."

"Jack Hicks?" I said. "I'm not sure."

"A good strong-sounding name. *Have you seen Jack Hicks around?*"

"Or *Is that Jack Hicks good-looking or what?*" I said, smiling.

"Or *Doctor Jack Hicks, Brain Surgeon.*"

I shook my head. "I like the name *Bobby*."

"So do I," Tina said. "So do I."

After a while we started to walk off the footbridge in the direction of the bus stop. We were going to the police station. Tina wanted to put things right and I wanted to be there to tell my part of the story.

After that she was going to go home and talk to her mum.

Milly was excited. So were the twins. Beverly watched as they ran up and down the hallway asking when the lady was coming.

"Don't worry," said Milly. "When Tina gets here me and the twins will go to the park. A couple of the others are around but if I know them they'll stay in their rooms. Come on you two, out and play in the garden for a while."

Beverly was apprehensive. From upstairs she could hear the strains of the trumpet. It was making her nerves stand on end. That and the twins' endless chatter and questions. She shouldn't be like this. She was professional. She'd handled these situations before. She went into Milly's big kitchen and found a chair to sit on. She picked out a file from her bag and placed it on the table. Next to it were pieces from Milly's china tea set which she had retrieved from a top cupboard and laid out ready for use. The cups were cream with rose patterns and the teapot was shapely with a fluted lid and a spout that looked like a lady's arm.

"Look at this lovely tea set. It's only used for important guests," Milly said, bending over Bobby.

Beverly smiled and continued to look through her papers. The baby was in his carrier at the other end of the long table. He was wearing a white babygro with red piping round the neck and cuffs. On his hands he had tiny cotton mittens. *To stop him scratching his face with his nails*, Milly explained when Beverly asked.

Beverly put her papers down and stepped across to talk to him.

"An important visitor for you, Bobby," she whispered.

He was almost three weeks old and seemed a little bigger every day. Instead of appearing fragile and worried, he now looked more confident, as if he was sure he had come to the right place. His eyes stared straight at her, searching her out. Beverly couldn't help but smile and with her finger she stroked his cheek, her fingernail, long and silver, barely touching his skin.

"What time are they coming?" Milly said, gathering some things in a stripy bag.

"About ten," Beverly said, looking at her watch.

"The grandmother as well?"

Beverly nodded. She flicked open her file.

"Marilyn Hicks. Thirty-nine years old. Suffers from depression. Married to the man who fathered her daughter's baby. Not exactly the best start for Bobby here."

"It's been decided that Bobby will live with his mother?"

"Not quite. There's a lot to discuss before that."

She turned to Bobby and said, "For now though, Mister, you're living with Milly."

"But in the long run?"

"We'll keep our fingers crossed. It's what we want, the baby with his mum. But we'll have to see how things work out."

Beverly bent forward over Bobby's carrier and gave him a light peck on the forehead. Her earrings, in the shape of triangles, swung forward and she held them back with her hands.

"And there'll be twice-weekly visits?"

Beverly nodded. The sound of the front doorbell made her stop and look round.

"That's them," she said.

Milly went to the back door and called the twins. They came tumbling in. From upstairs came the sound of a marching tune on the trumpet. The bell rang again.

"Remember, you can say hello to the baby's mum but then we're going to the park?" Milly said, wiping each of the twins' faces with wet wipes

Beverly went out to the hallway. She could hear Milly's voice listing the things that the twins were going to do at the park. She patted her hair and felt her nerves fade. She was in charge here. She had to help this situation go well. A lot depended on this meeting; for the mother and the grandmother. And for Bobby, of course. She opened the front door.

"Hello, Tina. Hello, Mrs Hicks. Nice to see you both again."

It looked as though two young girls were standing there. One thin, with short hair and deep circles under her eyes. The other not so tall, but well built, her hair pulled back, her face pretty with dark eyes and pale skin. Neither of them looked as though they'd had a good night's sleep for a while. Mrs Hicks was wearing trousers and a long-sleeved shirt. She had a large bag over her shoulder that had a plastic carrier bag sticking out of it. A present for the baby, no doubt. Tina was holding a mobile phone, passing it from one hand to the other.

"Come in, come in."

Beverly stood back to let them pass and pointed to the kitchen.

"Bobby's in there," she said, as the twins ran forward, firing questions at Tina and her mum.

"Come on, you lot, we're off to the park now."

"This is Milly. She's been looking after your baby."

Tina opened her mouth to speak but didn't say anything. She seemed rooted to the spot, her eyes fixed on the baby carrier on the table.

"Thank you," Mrs Hicks suddenly said, walking forward to shake hands with Milly. "I can't thank you enough for looking after the baby!"

"It's been a pleasure," Milly said, taking each twin

by a hand and walking out into the hall. Beverly followed her.

"What do you think?" Milly said, at the door. "Will they manage it?"

"I hope so!" Beverly said.

When Milly left she stood in the hallway for a moment. A face looked down at her from the top landing. A young teenage boy was standing there holding a trumpet. Beverly gave him a smile and he nodded and disappeared from view. In the kitchen she could just see the two women's backs as they leaned over the baby carrier. There was whispering going on and Beverly thought she heard a nervous laugh coming from Mrs Hicks.

She walked into the kitchen to join the three of them.

CHAPTER TWENTY-FOUR

Kath was coming to tea.

A week had passed since Tina and I had gone to the police. I'd talked to Kath on the phone but not seen her. She was busy, she said. She had a full week of shifts and she was also seeing her nurse mentor to discuss the events of the last weeks. I didn't envy her.

I got home from shopping just after six. I had a carrier bag full of food from the supermarket delicatessen, the kind of things that Kath liked: olives, salad, smoked meat. Not a chip in sight.

I found a Post-it stuck to the hall mirror.

Am picking the tickets up from the travel agents. Could you start the tea? Luv Mum xxx

I unpacked the food in the kitchen and thought about the holiday we were about to go on. A week in Crete. A last-minute bargain. There were new clothes hanging in my wardrobe waiting to be packed, a new swimsuit and flip-flops. In the bathroom were three giant bottles of sun cream, factor twenty.

I need this holiday, my mum had said, *I've been working too hard.*

What she really meant was that she needed to take me away on holiday. To get me away from the events of the past weeks. When I finally told her about the baby and the things we'd done she'd been horrified. Her words, *Why didn't you tell me?* rang in my ears for days. *How could you not tell me what was going on?*

I hadn't expected her to take the whole thing so personally.

I tried to explain. When she came home from work that night I tried to describe what had happened.

"I couldn't tell you, Mum, because Tina made me promise to keep it a secret. She didn't want anyone to know. I wasn't even supposed to tell Kath. . ."

"But you did tell Kath, and you didn't tell me!" she said, taking her work jacket off and hanging it round the back of a kitchen chair.

"Kath is a nurse. I thought she'd be able to give Tina medical advice. You're a parent. You're Marilyn's friend. I couldn't tell you."

She was brushing the shoulders of her jacket with her hand.

"I thought you and me could talk about anything!" she said.

"If I'd told you you would have made Tina go to the doctor's. You would have told Marilyn. Be honest. You would have. That's what parents do. They do the *right thing* even if it's not always the right thing to do at the time!"

I was getting confused. I knew what I meant. My mum took the jacket off the chair and patted the pockets as though she was looking for something.

"I could have helped," she said.

"But not in the way that Tina wanted."

She dropped the jacket on to the table and sat down heavily.

"I couldn't tell you, Mum!"

"Poor Marilyn," she said.

We had the conversation a number of times. In the end she booked a holiday and only told me about it when she got back from the travel agents. It was as if she was taking control of me again. I didn't mind. The responsibilities of the last weeks had worn me down.

I laid out the food on the table and heard the front door open.

"I'm back," my mum's voice sang out.

She came into the kitchen holding the tickets in mid-air.

"The day after tomorrow. You and me. On a plane to Crete."

I was glad. A week on the beach before I went back to school. It was just what I needed.

Kath bustled into the kitchen a while later.

"Um, olives," she said. "And hummus. Wonderful."

It was over a week since I'd seen her. She was wearing a loose blouse over some cut-off jeans and she looked really good. Her hair had been trimmed and her skin had its rosy hue back.

"Sorry I'm a bit late. I popped across the road," she said.

"How's Marilyn?" my mum said.

"And Tina?" I said.

"They're all right, considering. They saw the baby yesterday. They're full of it, telling me things like weight and height and all that stuff. Like I need to know!" Kath did a mock yawn. "Like I wasn't the one that pulled that baby into the world!"

"Um." My mum pursed her lips. She wasn't comfortable talking about it in any kind of light-hearted way.

"They've got a film of photos being developed so no doubt you'll see the little lad."

I coughed. "I have seen him already, remember."

My mum turned away and busied herself by cutting up some bread.

"They've also got this tiny babygro. The woman who's looking after him gave it to them. It's a Manchester United one, red and white. It's so *small*."

"What about you?" my mum said, her voice serious. "Are you going to get an official reprimand?"

Kath shook her head. Even though the police had kept the full details out of the newspapers the hospital authorities had been angry. Kath had taken equipment from the wards and used it. She'd been present at a birth and failed to notify a doctor. She'd disposed of clinical waste, breaking any number of hospital rules. In the end it had turned out all right but it could easily have ended in tragedy, they said.

"My mentor, Caroline, she says they're going to monitor me, send me on a course, have regular discussions with me but they're not going to put anything on my file or withdraw any of my nursing credits. She says the fact that it was me who contacted the police has helped. Not that it really mattered in the long run because Tina went herself . . . in the end."

I couldn't imagine what Kath would have done with herself if she hadn't kept her job. I watched her as she tucked into the salad and the meat and then took a great gulp from her glass of wine. She'd been a real friend.

The night before I went to Crete I walked across the road to Tina's. Marilyn opened the door and gave me a warm smile. Since the baby news had come out I had become an honorary member of the family. She had given me a couple of hugs and I had responded feeling a bit awkward, her thin arms exerting a powerful grip, her lips brushing my cheek, leaving a trace of lipstick.

I followed her down the hallway in the direction of the garden. She'd pulled her short hair up into a kind of ponytail and there were strands of it falling out and curling around her neck.

Tina was sitting on one end of a wooden bench with her feet up on a low table. On her lap was a ring-binder full of plastic folders. On the front, on a neat label, was the word *History*. The rest of the bench was full up with handouts and piles of A4 paper covered in handwriting and swathes of highlighter pen.

"Hi!" I said, looking quizzically at the paperwork which was flapping gently in the breeze.

"Grab a seat," she said, lifting her feet from the table.

I sat down as she placed the ring-binder on the bench with the rest of her stuff. I noticed, by her side, a small blue teddy bear, not unlike the one she used to have hanging off her rucksack.

"Just one of the many things that Mum's bought," she explained.

Further down the garden Marilyn was squatting in front of a flower bed pulling out weeds, pushing hair from her forehead with the back of her hand. She looked thinner somehow, and yet there was something busy about her, as if she had a task that had to be done by a certain time.

"All ready to fly off to Crete?" Tina said, cheerfully.

"I'm packed. Mum's brought plenty of factor twenty so I don't suppose I'll be getting a tan!" I said. "What you up to?"

"I'm going back to school," she said, looking pleased with herself.

"School?" I said, surprised.

She nodded. "I'm going to finish my A levels. And then start nursing."

"What about *the baby*?" I said, lowering my voice slightly, eyeing Marilyn further down the garden.

"I'm doing it for Bobby. If I'm going to be his mum I've got to have an education and a good job. I can't be one of those teenage mums who sit at home and do nothing . . . and expect everyone else to look after me. I'm not going to do that."

Tina glanced sideways to where her mum was and then looked quickly back at me.

"I've got to be strong. I've got to have a job. The job I wanted. I'm going to be a nurse."

"And the baby?"

"You mean *Bobby*?" she said smiling. "Beverly Ward – she's my social worker – she says it'll be a while before I can bring Bobby home. Me and mum, we've got to show them that we can provide a stable home for him, that we're not, I mean *I'm* not, going to suddenly change my mind again. It could be months."

Tina was silent, her mouth tightly shut. She seemed on the brink of saying something but didn't. Instead she picked up her ring-binder and ran her finger round the outside. She cleared her throat.

"So meanwhile I have to study. I can visit Bobby every other day and in a couple of weeks he can come and stay for the weekend. We have to take it slowly, Beverly says. And when he comes home for good then Mum's going to help and I'll look into nurseries and childminding. Stuff like that. Other people do it. Greg emailed me and told me that his cousin did a degree in Maths and Physics and she had a baby."

"Greg?" I said, bemused, remembering the nerdy lad from the grammar school.

"We keep in touch," Tina said, with a small smile.

"Look, Tine!" Marilyn called.

We both looked at her. She was standing by the shed at the end of the garden, holding a surfboard. It stood, taller than her, covered in bright, wavy lines; green, yellow and red.

"Ray bought it for her," Tina said. "She never did learn to surf."

"Does Ray know about Bobby?"

Tina shook her head.

"Not yet. In time he might. When we're all a bit stronger."

I looked down the garden. Marilyn had dropped the surfboard on to the grass and she was standing on it, her knees bent, her arms out, swaying from side to side as if she were riding a wave. I heard her laughing and looked back to see Tina licking her finger and counting out pages of A4 paper.

By her side was a small blue teddy bear that was just waiting to be played with. I left them in the garden and went home.

Don't miss

looking for jj

Everyone was looking for Jennifer Jones. She was dangerous, the newspapers said. She posed a threat to children and should be kept behind bars. The public had a right to know where she was. Some of the weekend papers even resurrected the old headline: *A Life for a Life!*

Alice Tully read every article she could find. Her boyfriend, Frankie, was bemused. He couldn't understand why she was so fascinated. He put his arm around her shoulder and dipped his mouth into her neck while she was reading. Alice tried to push him away but he wouldn't take no for an answer and in the end the newspaper crumpled and slipped on to the ground.

Alice couldn't resist Frankie. He was bigger and taller than her, but that wasn't difficult. Most people were. Alice was small and thin and often bought her clothes cheaply in the children's section of clothes shops. Frankie was a giant beside her, and liked to pick her up and carry her around, especially if they were having an argument. It was his way of making up.

She was lucky to have him.

She much preferred to read the articles about Jennifer Jones when she was on her own. It meant waiting until Rosie, the woman she lived with, was out at work. It gave her plenty of time. Rosie worked long hours. She was a social worker and had a lot of clients to see. In any case the stories about Jennifer

Jones weren't around all the time. They came in waves. Sometimes they roared from the front page, the headlines bold and demanding. Sometimes they were tiny, a column on an inside page, a nugget of gossip floating on the edge of the news, hardly causing a ripple of interest.

When the killing first happened the news was in every paper for months. The trial had thrown up dozens of articles from all angles. The events on that terrible day at Berwick Waters. The background. The home life of the children. The school reports. The effects on the town. The law regarding children and murder. Some of the tabloids focused on the seedier side: the attempts to cover up the crime; the details of the body; the lies told by the children. Alice Tully hadn't seen any of these at the time. She had been too young. In the past six months, though, she had read as much as she could get her hands on, and the question that lay under every word that had ever been printed was the same. How could a ten-year-old girl kill another child?

In the weeks leading up to the ninth of June, Alice Tully's seventeenth birthday, the stories started again. Jennifer Jones had finally been released. She had served six years for murder (the judge had called it *manslaughter* but that was just a nice word). She had been let out on licence which meant that she could be called back to prison at any time. She had been relocated somewhere far from where she was brought up. She had a new identity and no one would know who she was and what she had done.

Alice fell hungrily on these reports, just as she sat coiled up and tense in front of Rosie's telly, using her thumb to race past the satellite channels, catching every bit of footage of the Jennifer Jones case. The news programmes still used the only photograph that there had ever been of the ten year old. A small girl with long hair and a fringe, a frowning expression on her face. JJ was the little girl's nickname. The journalists loved it. It made Alice feel weak just to look at it.

On the morning of her birthday Rosie woke her up with a birthday card and present.

"Here, sleepyhead."

Alice opened her eyes and looked upwards at Rosie. She had her dark suit on and the white striped blouse she always wore with it. Her hair was tied back off her face, making her look serious and stern. Instead of her usual hanging earrings she was wearing gold studs. It was not the way Rosie liked to dress.

"Don't tell me, you're in court today!" Alice said, sitting up, stretching her arms out, ruffling her fingers through her own short hair.

"You guessed it!" Rosie said. "Here, take this, birthday girl!"

Alice took the present while Rosie walked to the window and pushed it open. A light breeze wafted in, lifting the net curtains. Alice pulled the duvet tight, up to her neck.

"Do you want to freeze me to death?" she said, jokingly.

Rosie took no notice. She loved fresh air. She spent a lot of her time opening windows and Alice spent a lot of time closing them.

Inside the wrapping paper was a small box, the kind that held jewellery. For a moment Alice was worried. Rosie's taste in jewellery was a bit too arty for her. She lifted the lid off gingerly and saw a pair of tiny gold earrings.

"These are lovely," Alice said and felt a strange lump in her throat.

"More your taste than mine," Rosie said, looking in Alice's wall mirror and pulling at her jacket, using the flats of her hands to smooth out her skirt. She looked uncomfortable.

Alice got out of bed and stood beside her. She held an earring up to one ear and nodded approvingly. Then she squeezed Rosie's arm.

"You're on lates this week?" Rosie said.

Alice nodded. She didn't have to be at work until ten.

"I'll be home early. So I'm going to cook a special meal," Rosie said. "And it's not only your birthday we're celebrating. Next Saturday, you'll have been here for six months!"

That was true. Six months of waking up every morning in that bedroom, of eating in Rosie's kitchen, of seeing her name on letters: *Alice Tully, 52 Phillip Street, Croydon.*

"My mum's coming. What about Frankie?"

Rosie had been making a special cake that had been hidden from Alice. Her mother Kathy, a funny Irish woman, was helping her.

"He can't come."

She didn't bother to explain. Frankie said he felt awkward around Rosie, as though she was watching him, waiting to tell him off every time he touched Alice. He preferred it when they were alone.

"Oh well. It'll be just the three of us then."

After Rosie left Alice sat on her bed holding the earrings and looking at her card. There would be nothing from her mother, she knew that. She sat very still for a moment, aware of her own body, trying to read her own sensations. Was she upset? She had other presents and cards. She had Frankie and her friends from the *Coffee Pot*. Then there was Rosie herself. Rosie with her powerful hug and no-nonsense manner; Rosie who smelled of lemons and garlic and basil and who was always trying to fatten her up. Dear, sweet Rosie. Alice hadn't known that such people existed.

The sound of the letterbox distracted her. She got up and took her card over to the mantelpiece and stood it up. Then she walked downstairs to the front door where the morning paper was sticking through the letterbox. She pulled it out, taking care not to graze it or tear the pages, and took it back up to the kitchen. Without looking she laid it down on the kitchen table and got on with making her breakfast. She tipped out some cereal and poured milk into her bowl. One dessertspoon of sugar was all she wanted. Then she got out the orange juice and poured herself exactly half a glass. Where eating was concerned she had a routine. She wasn't fussed about her weight or her shape. She just ate what she wanted and no amount of persuasion from anyone was going to change that.

She sat down and flattened the newspaper. There it was again, the headline she had expected.

JENNIFER JONES FREE AFTER SIX YEARS
Is this justice?

Her wrist trembled as she lowered her spoon into the bowl and scooped up some cereal. The story was the same as every other one that she had read over the last weeks. *Should Jennifer have been released? Should she stay in Britain? Is she a danger to children?* Then there was the revenge angle: *Would the dead girl's parents try to find Jennifer?*

As ever, the newspaper gave a brief outline of the story of that day at Berwick Waters. Alice read it. It was just like all the others. She had read them all. If anyone had asked she could have probably recited it by heart.

A bright blue day in May, six years before. The sun was staring down from the sky but a sharp breeze bothered the bushes and flowers, bending them this way and that. When it died down, the sun's glare was heavy, and for a fleeting moment it might have seemed like a midsummer day.

The town of Berwick. A few kilometres off the main Norwich road. It had a high street with shops and a pub and road after road of neatly laid-out houses and gardens. Beyond the small school and the park the road led out of the town past the disused railway station to Water Lane. A row of cottages, eight of them. Formerly owned by the council, they stood in a small orderly line along the road.

They weren't all run-down. Some were cared for, with conservatories and extensions built on. Others had peeling paint and broken fences. Some of the gardens were colourful and neat, their blooms in geometric beds, their terracotta pots standing upright, early blossoms tumbling over the edges. Others were wild with weeds and strewn with broken toys. Above them all were washing lines hoisted up into the sky, children's shirts and dresses struggling in the breeze one minute and hanging limply in the sun the next.

Three children emerged from a gate at the back of one of the gardens and started on the path to Berwick Waters. It was only a kilometre and a half away and they were walking smartly, as though they had some purpose. The lake at Berwick Waters was man-made, filled up some ten years before by the water company. It was over three kilometres long and was surrounded by woodland and some landscaped picnic areas. The water in the lake was deep and children were not encouraged to go there alone. Some people said that families of feral cats had lived in the area and had been drowned when it was filled. At times, during the day, when there was absolute silence, some people said, their cries could be heard. Most people dismissed this, but many children were in awe of the story.

On that day in May the children were cold at first, that's why they were hugging themselves, pulling the sleeves of their jumpers down, trying to keep the niggling breeze from forcing its way inside their clothes. Five minutes later it was too hot and the jumpers came off and ended up tied round their waists, each garment holding tightly on to its owner. Three children walked away from the cottages on the edge of the town towards Berwick Waters. Later that day only two of them came back.

Alice Tully knew the story. She could have written a book about it.

She looked at her cereal bowl and saw that she'd eaten only half of it. She picked up her spoon and continued, chewing vigorously, swallowing carefully, hardly tasting a mouthful. At the bottom of the editorial there was a final quote from an official at the Home Office:

"Like any other offender Jennifer Jones has been carefully vetted. It was the considered opinion of all those concerned that she poses no threat to children and accordingly she was released under licence and is currently living in a safe environment. Any talk of revenge or vigilante action is wholly inappropriate and will be dealt with in the most rigorous manner."

Where was Jennifer Jones? That's what everyone was saying. There were only a handful of people in the country who knew. Alice Tully was one of them.